THE FIFTH URBAN FARM FRESH ROMANCE

Flavors of Forever

VALERIE COMER

GreenWords Media

ACKNOWLEDGMENTS

Thank you for being a faithful reader of the Urban Farm Fresh Romance series!

Thanks to Elizabeth Maddrey, first reader and idea-bouncer. You talked me off the ledge a few times in the midst of this challenging story. I appreciate your encouragement and (usually) gentle boots to the backside. Also thank you to beta readers Tina and Paula for your valuable insights and help in making this story so much stronger.

A big thank you to my fabulous editor, Nicole, who sees beyond words, punctuation, and sentence structure to the heart of the story.

I'm also grateful for the Christian Indie Authors Facebook group and my sister bloggers at Inspy Romance. These folks make a difference in my life every single day. I'm thrilled to walk beside them as we tell stories for Jesus!

Thank you to my Facebook friends, followers, street team, and reader group members for prayers, encouragement, and great fellowship. Thanks to to my email subscribers for coming through with many worship song playlist additions while thinking about the reckless, wild, steadfast, forever love of God.

Thanks to my husband, Jim, for research trips to Spokane and talking through scenarios as needed — to say nothing of everyday love and support — and to my kids and grandgirls for cheering me on and embracing the idiosyncrasies of having an author for a mom and grandmother.

All my love and gratitude goes to Jesus, the One who invited me to experience His unending and passionate love and walks beside me every day. My prayer is that you see His love anew through the pages of this story.

Valerie Comer Bibliography

Urban Farm Fresh Romance

0. Promise of Peppermint (ebook only)
1. Secrets of Sunbeams
2. Butterflies on Breezes
3. Memories of Mist
4. Wishes on Wildflowers
5. Flavors of Forever
6. Raindrops on Radishes
7. Dancing at Daybreak

Saddle Springs Romance

1. The Cowboy's Christmas Reunion
2. The Cowboy's Mixed-Up Matchmaker
3. The Cowboy's Romantic Dreamer
4. The Cowboy's Convenient Marriage

Christmas in Montana Romance

1. More Than a Tiara
2. Other Than a Halo
3. Better Than a Crown

Garden Grown Romance
(Arcadia Valley Romance)

1. Sown in Love (ebook only)
2. Sprouts of Love
3. Rooted in Love
4. Harvest of Love

Farm Fresh Romance

1. Raspberries and Vinegar
2. Wild Mint Tea
3. Sweetened with Honey
4. Dandelions for Dinner
5. Plum Upside Down
6. Berry on Top

Riverbend Romance Novellas

1. Secretly Yours
2. Pinky Promise
3. Sweet Serenade
4. Team Bride
5. Merry Kisses

valeriecomer.com/books

*C*ouldn't she rub her aching feet *yet*? Crawl up the stairs at the back of Bridgeview Bakery and Bistro to the apartment she shared with her cousin and co-owner?

Kassidy North turned back to the brightly lit, teeming space. Her smile faltered when her gaze swept the clock. Two more hours until closing.

"Girl, this is a happening place!" Former employee Linnea Ranta — no, Linnea Dermott now — bumped Kass's elbow. "This birthday party is such a success you've got a line out the door."

Kass groaned. "Tell me that's not true."

"Oh, it's true, all right." Linnea glanced around. "Where's all the staff?"

"Shay put in her eight hours and couldn't stay. Ava broke her leg day before yesterday. The new girl... well, let's just say she's a warm body, but the tables are getting cleared at least. Hailey's in the kitchen taking more cinnamon rolls out of the oven, so that leaves me on everything else."

"Where's an apron?" Linnea stepped past Kass to the hooks beside the office door.

"But you don't work here anymore." Kass couldn't help the lilt of hope that infused her words before guilt set in. After all, Linnea and Logan had returned from their honeymoon just a day or two ago and were packing for their move to Seattle.

"I work here today." Linnea tied the apron around her back. "Where can I do the most good?"

Kass heaved a sigh of relief. "Running the till. I'll plate."

Linnea nodded and turned to the next person in line. "Hi there. What would you like?"

"I've heard I can order bread and stuff for weekly pickup, but the rack with sign-up forms is empty."

Kass snagged the notebook off the counter. "I'll help you over here." At least Linnea could keep the line moving while she took time out. And hadn't they printed enough of those order forms? The rack had been jammed full at seven this morning.

"Logan can do that. He's familiar with all the inventory." Linnea waved both arms to catch her husband's attention from where he sat at a table chatting with some of their friends. When he looked up, she beckoned him over.

"You've got him well trained already," Kass whispered to her friend.

Linnea grinned as she tugged the notebook out of Kass's hands and pressed it into Logan's. "Would you mind helping out with standing orders, love? You know the drill."

He should. Logan had worked his way through the entire menu in the year or so he'd lived in the neighborhood before settling into a weekly subscription of his favorites. The man did not love to cook.

"No problem." Logan looked at the notebook, snagged a pen from the holder beside the cash register, and smiled at the forty-something woman who stood there looking from one to the other. "As you can see, ma'am, baked goods from Bridgeview Bakery and Bistro are in high demand, but I know we can fill your order. Let's take a seat over here." He led the woman over to the table where he'd been having coffee and shooed the other guys out of their chairs.

Kass dared to breathe. Maybe they'd survive today after all. Thank the Lord tomorrow was Sunday, and they'd be able to relax. She hadn't promised to bring snacks for coffee time at church, had she? Pretty sure that was next week. She'd check her reminder app later... if she remembered.

Linnea clipped an order to the line, and Kass glanced at it before scooping a bowl of sausage and kale chowder then placing a warm sourdough biscuit beside it. A pat of butter, and the plate went up.

She settled into the routine, breathing a prayer of thanks for Linnea's and Logan's help. Hailey slid a pan of warm cinnamon rolls into the display case, and a few patrons who'd already been seated returned to sample the sweet treats.

"Three years in business? Congratulations. That's an achievement these days." An older man Kass didn't remember seeing before smiled as he accepted a plate with four chewy chocolate peppermint cookies. "These smell really good."

"Thank you." Kass glanced at the order. "Your London Fog will be right up." She turned to the machine.

"The guys from my office told me about this hidden gem. I'm impressed. Really impressed."

"We've been blessed."

"Interesting choice of words."

"Our grandparents operated a bakery here years ago and willed it to my cousin and me. It was a lot of work to bring it up to code and re-open, but it's been worth it." A lot of work and a lot of cash. "We've dedicated this business to God, asking Him to bless our community through us."

The man waved a hand. "Looks like a lot of people are being *blessed*, as you put it. At least they seem happy to be here."

Hailey had turned off the music hours ago. It had been drowned by the sounds of voices and laughter anyway. A quick peek around the vibrant café brought a grin to Kass's face. "It's been a good day. Here's your drink, sir. Thank you for coming in, and I hope to see you again sometime."

"I'm sure you will."

Tiny interludes like this had taken place all day, making everything worthwhile. She and Hailey had prayed God would bless their business and grow it, and He'd sent Nathan Hamelin, a marketing guru who'd grown up here in Spokane and learned his trade in L. A., to ignite plans for this third-birthday extravaganza.

Nathan had even helped cover the noon rush, citing his college years waiting on tables. Now the newlyweds were pitching in. What had she and Hailey done to deserve such good friends? And what were they going to do if even a fraction of today's visitors came back?

The crash of shattering china yanked Kass from the monotony of fixing lattes and plating sweets while smiling, nodding, and greeting an endless sea of faces.

Across the counter stood a man with dusky blond hair and a neatly trimmed short beard clutching the hand of his mini-me. The boy, about seven, stared up at Kass with his eyes wide and his mouth in an 'o.' "I'm s-sorry."

Kass pushed a smile to the front. "It's okay." She grabbed the broom and dustpan from inside the closet and rounded the counter. Oh, no. A platter lay in shards.

She bent to clean up the mess, only then recognizing the platter, one of the few that had remained from her grandparents' days in the bakery. Grandma had served tea and cookies to two little girls on matching floral china. The citrusy aroma of the lemon squares on the tile floor morphed into the bergamot tea and snowdrop cookies dusted in confectioners' sugar from her childhood.

Kass blinked away both the tears and the desire to bolt up the back stairs and hide out for even a little while.

WESLEY FERGUSON STARED at the fragments of duck egg blue china on the tiles at his feet. Had that been a vintage piece? If he didn't miss his guess, a Tuscan Works design from Staffordshire in the mid-forties. Yes, that shard was a gilded ear handle. Oh, man, the thing was rare. Priceless.

Shattered.

"I d-didn't mean to, Daddy."

Wesley Ferguson pulled his son closer. "I know, buddy." But sorry wasn't enough, and there was no way he could afford to replace the plate... and that's if a replacement existed on the planet.

Did the redhead who crouched in front of him know? The gorgeous woman who, incidentally, had no diamond on her finger? He touched her shoulder. "I'm so sorry. Here, let me get that."

Another woman approached with a small cardboard

box, and Wesley took it then squatted by the aromatic mess.

The redhead sniffed. "I've got it." She swept the larger pieces together, the turquoise border laced with white flowers.

"It's the least I can do. That was a rare piece. I'm so sorry my son bumped into it." He picked up the gilded handle, set it in the box, and reached for another.

She dumped a dustpanful into the box and cast him a sidelong glance.

Wesley winced at the clatter of broken glass. "Easy does it."

"They're already broken." Moisture glistened in her brown eyes.

"Maybe it can be repaired."

Her eyebrows rose. "There are dozens of pieces."

As though he couldn't see that. "Let me try."

The clamor of voices and laughter continued unabated around them, but the only things pulling his thoughts away from the pretty woman were Sebastian's pointy elbow digging into his shoulder and the mess in front of them.

"I'm Kassidy North," she said at last, searching his face. "My cousin and I own this café."

"Wesley Ferguson. I'd like to say it's nice to meet you, but not like this. My son, Sebastian, and I just moved into the neighborhood." He stretched out his hand.

She looked at her lemon-custard-covered fingers and shook her head.

"I'm s-so sorry."

"It's okay." Kassidy eyed his boy then angled slightly away. "I'll clean this up. Don't worry about it. Had you already placed your order? Linnea would be happy to help you at the counter." She dumped two quick pans into the box.

Dismissed, then. She didn't even ask how he knew the piece, how he thought he might repair it. Not that it would be exactly the same.

The gum-chewing waitress he'd noticed earlier leaned over his shoulder. "Now there's a mess."

Kassidy looked up. "Celeste? Can you get a bucket and rag and finish here, please?"

The young woman nodded. "You got it."

Wesley rose and pulled Sebastian further from the diminishing disaster. His son tugged him to a nearby display case. "Can we get a c-cinnamon roll?"

"Sure, buddy, but they're huge. Split one with you?"

"Okay."

He placed his order, along with milk for Sebastian and a coffee for himself, before retreating to a table just being vacated by several teens, where he sat facing into the cheerfully decorated bistro. The waitress wiped up the remains of the lemon squares while, behind the counter, Kassidy washed her hands then turned to help the next customer.

"This is g-good," whispered Sebastian.

Wesley grinned at his son. "It is. I'm glad our neighbors told us to come here, aren't you?" Not that he hadn't seen the posters announcing the birthday party around their new community, but the personal recommendation from the Sheridans next door had been the final nudge.

This was his kind of building. Exterior walls of reclaimed brick met the inner walls' whitewashed planks. Chairs painted in yellow, white, and turquoise surrounded wooden tables, similar colors popping up in signage and a few antiques. The duck egg blue platter had been right at home... and should have been kept well out of the hubbub. Although, Sebastian shouldn't have reached for one of the lemon squares sitting on it, either.

His gaze lingered on Kassidy North. Her red hair had been braided from the crown of her head and ended past her shoulder blades. Sydney had always hated fiddling with her hair, keeping it short and spiked.

Sydney. Sebastian hadn't talked about his mom in a while, and Wesley had done his best to push thoughts of her out of his mind. She'd promised him forever, but her definition had been different than his.

Sydney would have reacted a lot differently than Kassidy had to a broken heirloom. Good grief — she'd freaked out when Sebastian dropped a Corelle bowl.

"Dad, th-this looks good."

Wesley pulled his gaze from the redhead back to his

son, who pointed at a paper. "What's that?" He picked up the pamphlet with a photo of a casserole on the front. A once-a-month cooking club? He chuckled. That's about how often he got struck by inspiration but, wait, that's not what this was about. Instead, it was about a group cooking experience where each participant took home twenty meals for their family every month. Twenty meals. Five days a week, he'd know what was for supper.

His interest mounted as he explained the concept to Sebastian. "I don't know if you'd like it, buddy. There's chili and lasagna and..." He flipped the pamphlet over and his voice stopped working.

"I like ch-chili."

Kassidy's smiling face met his from the photo on the paper. She was the facilitator? Seemed so. Her email address. Her phone number.

He and Sebastian needed to eat, didn't they? Certainly there was more to life than hot dogs and takeout. He folded the pamphlet and stuck it in his shirt pocket. "Ready to go home? We have time to unpack a lot more boxes today. Maybe we can get your room finished up before bedtime."

Sebastian's face lit as he slid off his chair.

They walked out the door as a middle-aged couple set their cups on the vacated table. On a whim, Wesley guided Sebastian around the back of the building. Aha, just as he suspected. Beside the trash can sat the small cardboard box holding the fragments of Kassidy's vintage platter.

Wesley tucked it under his arm. He could create something beautiful out of it and give it back to her. It was only because he felt so badly about Sebastian's clumsiness. Right?

Sure, he could try convincing himself of that. Maybe it would even work.

CHAPTER 2

*D*on't make me move." Kass yanked her aching feet deeper under her duvet as her cousin, Hailey, tried to tickle them. "I'm staying in bed until supper."

"Church starts in an hour."

"I'm skipping today." She *never* skipped... and besides, how could Hailey sound so cheerful? They'd both put in a fourteen-hour day yesterday by the time the last dishwasher load had been run and all the counters, tables, and floors washed.

"No, you're not. It's where we go on Sunday mornings."

Kass squeezed her eyes shut. Every muscle in her body throbbed, and the headache she'd barely kept at bay still lingered. "I can't do it." There were a lot of things she couldn't do. Telling Hailey about the broken plate ranked right up there.

"Logan's playing piano for worship one last time, since they're moving on Friday. Also, you don't want to miss their farewell party."

The way her head felt? She definitely wanted to miss it. On the other hand, her cousin was right. Although Francesca Amato was a fine pianist, Fran and everyone else would miss Logan's effervescent style.

"I'll bring you some painkillers and a glass of water. Be right back." Hailey's footsteps disappeared and returned.

Kass struggled to sit up then downed the little pills. She eyed Hailey. "How come you're not as exhausted as I am?" It certainly wasn't that her cousin had left all the work to Kass.

Hailey shrugged, grinning. "I loved every minute of it, but we do need to hire more staff."

"You can say that again." Kass leaned against her pillows. "With Linnea gone and Ava's accident, we could use several flexible part timers. I don't want to go through a day like yesterday again."

"How can you say that? Tons of new customers came through the doors, and we made a pile of money. I hope they all come back."

"Just not at the same time. And not until we have more employees."

"Yeah, yeah. It'll be fine. We survived, didn't we?"

"More or less." Memories of yesterday's melee rolled through Kass's mind. Why on earth had she thought it would be a good idea to take the antique plate off its high, safe shelf and put lemon squares on it? It had been an impulsive decision, but the colors matched the display case she'd set it on so well. It had looked magnificent.

Sure, she owned it as much as Hailey did, since the entire contents of the building had gone to both of them, but her cousin placed more value on things like that. *Things*, in general.

Kass pushed the thoughts aside along with her duvet. Didn't look like she was getting out of leaving the apartment today, after all. She was too wide awake now to fall back asleep. And the first time she had a few minutes, she'd go downstairs and rearrange that shelf to negate the gap from the missing plate. Maybe she could find a replacement online before Hailey noticed it was missing.

Meanwhile, she'd drown her guilt in the shower.

⌒⌣

WESLEY NUDGED Sebastian into a pew toward the back of Bridgeview Bible Church. He wasn't much of a church-goer, not in recent years, anyway, but Myles Sheridan had invited him to this, too. Said the church was the heart of the Bridgeview community, so Wesley was doing this for his son. It would be good for Sebastian to meet some kids his age before school started later in August.

The loud, outgoing girl next door terrified his son.

Thankfully, she was a couple of years older and Sebastian wouldn't have to put up with her in class but, surely, there were other six-year-old boys in the neighborhood.

He looked around as people chatted in the aisles. There were a few gray heads, plenty of middle-aged folks, teens, young families with school-aged kids and babies. A thirtyish guy with shoulder-length blond hair took a seat at the baby grand, flexed his shoulders, and began to play.

Wesley's eyes widened. Man, did this guy play professionally? Wesley wasn't familiar with the song, but that made no difference. Talent oozed from the guy's flashing fingers as he commanded the entire keyboard. If he gave lessons, Wesley should sign Sebastian up.

The music seemed a cue for people to find their seats. In a few minutes, everyone sat expectantly quiet as a Latino man made his way to the front then adjusted the microphone. The pianist gentled the music, playing more softly.

"Welcome to Bridgeview Bible Church on this lovely summer morning. My name is Tomas Ramirez, and I'm the pastor. I'm so glad to see you here today. If I haven't had a chance to meet you yet, I hope you'll say hello after the service." His gaze zeroed straight at Wesley.

Wesley nodded slightly. He could do that. In fact, he was going to do everything right from now on. He'd have to, or Sydney's parents would challenge him for custody of Sebastian. The only reason they hadn't was lack of interest in moving out of their condo in a fifty-plus community. That, and Wesley's promise to move to Spokane. He was here now, for better or for worse.

For richer or for poorer. In sickness and in health... The wedding vows he'd once made continued to filter through his mind. Too bad Sydney hadn't really meant them, but Wesley had tried. Hadn't known how — not with his background — but he'd tried. Especially after their son's birth.

He shook his head as the pianist spoke into a microphone even while his fingers drifted across the keys. "Would you stand and join together in worshiping our Creator this morning?" And then he began to sing. Lyrics appeared on a screen beside the platform, and Wesley read the words as at least a hundred voices lifted together.

Forever God is faithful.

Was He? Really? Wesley had never thought so, but a glance around showed that these people believed it. Eyes closed, feet tapping, hands lifted... oh, not everyone stood like that, but Wesley couldn't see anyone who didn't seem immersed in the experience one way or another. Was it the command of the musician, or was there something more?

Motion caught his eye as the redhead he'd met yesterday hurried down the aisle with a blond-haired woman. Both edged into a row close to the front, greeted by friends with a smile and a touch. Adriana Sheridan leaned forward from the pew behind and patted Kassidy's shoulder.

Whatever was going on in this building caught at Wesley's heart. He hadn't been part of anything worthwhile for far too long. But now? He wanted roots for his son. For himself.

He tore his gaze from Kassidy back to the screen as the congregation exulted, "His love endures forever."

Okay. He'd be open to whatever happened here. He'd try, anyway.

⁂

AS THE SERVICE came to a close and Logan's final notes drifted to silence, Kass felt Hailey's elbow in her ribs. "Told you you wanted to come today."

"And you were right."

"Of course." Hailey smirked. "Also, did you see that new guy sitting toward the back on the other side? Blond. Gorgeous. Intense." She leaned closer. "I think he's staring at me."

Please, Lord, let someone fall in love with Hailey soon so she can stop chasing men and embarrassing her friends. It might not have been a charitable prayer, but that didn't make it less real.

"No, I was focused on my reason for being here. You know, worship. Listening to Pastor Tomas. Prayer."

"Puh-leeze. I can do all that and keep an eye out for

people new to church. Someone has to notice, so we can say hello and make sure he feels welcome. It's our duty, even." Hailey looked past Kass's shoulder, and her face pulled into a frown. "Or someone else can do it. He's got a kid. No wife in sight, though."

Kass couldn't resist a glance at her cousin's obvious cool-down. Wesley, one hand on Sebastian's shoulder, chatted with Marco Santoro. Then he caught sight of her and gave her a slight smile and nod.

She gripped Hailey's arm. "Oh, he came into the bistro yesterday. I think he's Adriana and Myles's new neighbor." She paused as if searching for the information, though she remembered every second of the encounter. "Um... Wesley, I think?" Now was not the time for going into how they'd met.

Hailey cast one more glance to the back then shrugged. "Come on. There's coffee and pastries downstairs."

Kass gathered her purse and Bible then followed Hailey toward the foyer.

"That was a happening party yesterday." Jasmine Santoro touched her arm as she passed. "Nathan and I drove by a couple of more times since we needed supplies for the renovation project at his house, and it looked like you were busy clear until closing."

Kass smiled at her friend. "It was a big success. And I am super tired, but I couldn't miss Linnea and Logan's going-away party today. They even pitched in at the bistro yesterday. I'll miss them both in more ways than I can count."

"I know. Me, too. The apartment already seems too quiet, and Linnea only moved out two weeks ago."

"Looking for another roommate?"

Jasmine shook her head, a small smile poking one cheek. "I'd planned to, but then Nathan asked me to marry him, so I'll only be living there a few more months." She sighed, eyes going soft.

Kass swallowed the stab of jealousy. Not because she'd had designs on Nathan, but because her friends seemed to be pairing off at a steady rate. Even Jasmine, who hadn't dated or seemed interested in it for as long as Kass had known her... until Nathan moved back to town. If some great guy came along and asked Kass out, how would she even get to know him? The café took all her time and energy.

Jasmine linked their arms and tugged her toward the stairs to the fellowship hall. "Your turn will come."

"Didn't you hate when people said that to you?"

"Um, yeah. Sorry. But having the new-and-improved Nathan back in Bridgeview... I guess I want all my friends to be as happy in love as I am."

They emerged into the basement room, where Nathan stood chatting with some of Jasmine's brothers. Jasmine hurried to her fiancé's side, but Kass stopped and looked around. It wasn't that the Santoro guys weren't nice enough. She counted them as friends — well, except for Basil, who was perpetually sardonic —

but she didn't feel a single fuzzy, heart-looping thought around any of them. Hanging around them too much would get church people speculating. Or, even worse, Bridgeview's ruling matriarch, Marietta, who was very opinionated about whom her grandsons dated.

Across the room, Wesley Ferguson still chatted with Marco, who happened to be Jasmine's only married brother. Both men had a hand on the shoulder of a little boy. Wesley seemed to be a good dad. A loving dad.

Kass stifled a grin as the two boys sized up the other one. Sebastian and Oren would either head to the playground to be best friends or pound each other out. Buddies would be better.

Wesley tipped his head back and laughed at something Marco said. Then Pastor Tomas approached, and Marco introduced them. Tomas and Juanita had a son about that age, too. See, those were the kinds of friends Wesley needed to make. Ones with boys the age of Sebastian.

Not a single woman who only yearned to improve the lives of motherless children. After her last venture at falling in love with a single dad, she'd vowed to stick to sending her tithe to orphanages in third world countries and teaching on rotation in junior church. Mason. He'd been in love with someone else before Kass even came on the scene. Someone he'd been trying to get over since it could never work. Well, it had worked, and he seemed happy when Kass ran into them at the church in Galena Landing on visits to her parents. Mason had held a baby boy on one arm with his wife tucked close beside him as he greeted Kass. The twins had hugged her, though.

"Kass! That was a great party yesterday." Daria, Marco's wife, gave her a quick squeeze. "Congratulations to you and Hailey. I knew you could build a thriving business."

"Thanks. We weren't sure there for a year or two if we were going to be able to pull it off, but with the kind of community support we received, it was possible."

"Well, you two are part of Bridgeview as your grandparents were, so of course we supported you. And now it seems all of Spokane has discovered you. That's awesome."

Kass took a deep breath. She should be a whole lot more excited than she was. "If you know of anyone looking for a job, we're hiring."

Daria laughed. "I bet you are. I'll keep it in mind." She angled a glance toward her husband, still chatting with Wesley and Tomas. Myles Sheridan had joined them. "Who's the new guy?"

Right, Daria had spent the last hour teaching junior church. "He came by the bistro for the party. Wesley something-or-other. That's all I know." All Kass was willing to share, not that she knew much more, really. She wasn't about to admit to anyone that the intensity in his blue eyes had left her so unsettled yesterday.

CHAPTER 3

*W*esley dumped the box of porcelain shards onto a large screen over a trash can.

"What are you doing, Daddy? C-can I help?" Big blue eyes peered up at him.

"I'm going to wash the lemon off these pieces and see what I've got to work with. How many pieces are big enough." He picked up the spray nozzle. "Can you run and turn the water on?"

Sebastian dashed off and, seconds later, Wesley felt the hose swell. He kinked it to limit the pressure then dribbled water over the sticky pile. Custard oozed away, along with the tiniest bits of china, leaving behind gleaming white and duck-egg-blue pieces.

Wesley picked out the biggest remnants. Of the four ears, only one was broken through. Excitement mounted as he arranged the fragments like puzzle pieces on a nearby board until he had a semblance of the plate's original shape. It had been a gorgeous piece. It would be again.

"It's p-pretty." Sebastian reached out.

"Don't touch, son. The pieces have very sharp edges. You might cut yourself."

"But you touched."

"Very carefully—"

"Yoo-hoo! What are you doing?"

Sebastian cringed as Wesley turned slowly to see the girl next door opening the gate between their two properties. Oh, no. Would anyone notice if he welded the latch shut? Apparently previous homeowners had been good friends. Or else the child simply had no boundaries.

"Hi Vi—"

"If you're looking for your cat, she's in our yard. Better watch out, or our dog will chase her. Maybe bite her."

"Him." Wesley found his voice. "Our cat is a boy, and his name is Taz."

Violet's face brightened. "Like the Tasmanian devil? That's a funny name. Our dog's Duke. He's a boy, too."

Duke was the size of a small pony. Adriana and Myles had introduced him as a Great Pyrenees crossed with a Labrador. Either way, Wesley was pretty sure Duke was too good-natured to take on a feisty little cat.

"D-don't let him eat Taz." Sebastian tugged at Wesley's T-shirt.

"He won't."

"But sh-she said..."

Wesley turned back to Violet. "Thanks for letting us know. I'm sure your dad will be looking for you soon, so you'd better scoot on home."

The little girl pushed her mop of hair out of her eyes as she leaned closer. "Mr. Myles isn't really my dad, you know. My real dad is in heaven because he died. He was a hero." She squinted at Sebastian. "Where's your mom? Is she in heaven, too?"

"She—" Wesley started.

"Heaven's a great place, Mom said. My dad is best friends with Jesus, you know. And he watches over me."

Was that even biblical? Wesley wasn't sure, but he'd heard sentiments like it often enough. As though Sydney sang with the angels and kept an eye on Sebastian. Right. Those hadn't been her strong points on earth.

Violet pressed closer until she was right in Sebastian's face. "Where's your mom?"

Wesley tugged his son behind him as he stepped in front of the nosy little girl. "Sebastian is kind of shy, and he doesn't like a lot of questions. How about you run along home now?"

The child looked puzzled. She probably didn't understand the concept of bashfulness. Her kind rarely did. "My mom doesn't need me for anything right now. She told me to go outside and play."

"I think she meant in your own yard, though." He pointed at the gate. "Sebastian and I are busy, so it's time for you to go."

"What're you doing?" She peered over at his makeshift workbench.

Wesley stifled a groan. He'd all but issued a direct command, well past a hint, and the kid was still here. "We're working on a project." Brilliance hit. "A lot of my projects involve dangerous, noisy machines, so you really shouldn't come in our yard without permission." Permission he'd never grant.

Violet tilted her head. "I don't hear anything."

"That's because we haven't started yet. Look, I'll come get Taz so he's out of your way, then you'll need to stay in your yard." He headed through the open gate, but the scruffy cat was nowhere to be seen.

Duke, sprawled in the shade by the large back deck, opened one eye and twitched an ear. Wesley smirked. Definitely a cat-eater.

"The cat was staring at the chickens. He better not bother them, or Sassy will peck at him."

At least Violet had followed him back to her yard. That was a huge bonus. Now if he could only find Taz.

Myles poked his head out of the garage. "Hey, neighbor. What can I do for you?"

Keep his kid at home? Er, stepchild. "Violet came

over to tell us Taz is in your yard, but I don't see him anywhere."

Myles crossed his arms and looked down at the girl. "Didn't we tell you not to go next door without an invitation?"

She glared up at him. "I thought he'd want to know about his cat."

"Cats can jump over fences and walk across on trees. You'll get used to seeing their cat around, and it's okay. Pets have different rules than kids."

Violet sighed. "But I'm bored, and Sam's reading."

Wesley had met the older child, a studious-looking boy quite unlike his sister.

"Makes no difference. Rules are rules." Myles crouched beside the girl.

"But you're not even my dad."

To his credit, Myles ruffled the girl's hair and laughed. "I am now. Your mom and I made the rule together, and we expect you to obey it. Promise me, Violet."

She scuffed her toe against the grass.

"Violet."

"Fine. I won't do it again. But I don't think it's fair their cat doesn't have that rule. Duke does."

One of the reasons Wesley had chosen the property was that it was a large lot bordering the river. If he had to live in a city, it needed to be on his terms, where deer might wander through and the sounds of nature predominated over traffic and sirens. He certainly didn't want to confine Taz to the house. Who wanted to clean a litter box if he didn't have to? Besides, Sebastian was forever forgetting to shut the screen door. Add *install self-closing hinge* to his ever-growing to-do list.

Violet huffed off, and Myles shook his head. "Sorry about that. Adriana and I have only been married a couple of months, and Violet's still got some adjusting to do. Some days I think I've won her over and, other days, I'm certain I never will."

"She..." Wesley searched for polite words. "She seems an interesting personality."

Myles chuckled. "She is, at that. What are you and Sebastian up to today? Want to come in for coffee? Adriana's baking up a storm in there, testing out recipes for a dinner party we're holding next weekend. I'm sure she'd be happy for an unbiased critique."

"Baking? In this weather?" Wesley glanced around to see Sebastian standing in the open gate. No sign of the cat. No sign of Violet, either. Maybe it wouldn't be too awkward.

"I know, right? She's running the air conditioner as well." Grinning, Myles shrugged. "Food makes her happy."

"Uh..." He'd promised himself he'd be a good neighbor. Make friends. Fit in. "Maybe for a few minutes." He beckoned Sebastian over.

"Great." Myles led the way up to the back deck.

"Is Adriana expecting you?" Kass asked Jasmine as they strolled down the riverfront path enjoying the lovely morning. The river's wild turmoil of early spring had settled to a gentle current now in August. "Because it looks like the perfect day for fishing. Wade said he caught two redbands a couple of days ago."

"We can get some angling in, for sure, but Adriana said to drop by any time." Jasmine twirled, arms wide. "Mom says it's time to talk wedding dresses. Adriana did such a gorgeous job on Eden's and Linnea's that of course I want her to sew mine, too. My mother has already started making the guest list and phoning venues and..."

"I get it. Your parents have four sons and only one daughter. They're going to do this up right." Still, a little something tweaked in Kass's gut. Jasmine was her most introverted and nature-oriented friend and could always be counted on for berry picking or fishing. Sounded like Kass might be on her own for such adventures in the future.

Jasmine stopped in mid-twirl. "Is it archaic to let your parents put on the wedding? I mean, Mom will let me have my way where I really care, but mostly she and Nonna have their heads together planning an extravagant party."

Would Kass's dad and stepmom do the same? Probably only if she wanted to get married in Galena Landing where she'd grown up. Bridgeview was home now, and all her friends were here. Not that it mattered, since weddings required grooms as well as brides, and there was no man in sight. She wouldn't think about that right now. She'd just be happy for Jasmine and Nathan, who'd found each other again after eight years apart.

The river tumbled along beside them, the cottonwoods and aspens providing mottled shade in this little piece of nature in the midst of Spokane. It didn't have the wildness of northern Idaho, but she'd grown to love it here, too.

"You'll be my maid of honor, won't you? I'm hoping Linnea and Logan will be back for Christmas holidays from college and can stand up for us, too."

"Sure—"

"Nathan wants Peter to be best man... is that okay? I keep wishing you and Peter would get together but, unless I'm completely blind, that doesn't seem to be happening, right?"

"Um, no. I like your cousin just fine, but there's no spark." Kass held up both hands. "And don't even start with your brothers."

"I don't know if you've dated at all since you moved to Bridgeview."

"Nope." Kass managed a chuckle. "There hasn't been time. Hailey and I worked so hard renovating the building and apartment, and then twice as hard every day in the three years we've been open. I fall into bed exhausted every night... by nine-thirty, if I can manage it." All that was true, but she'd also been trying to protect her heart after Mason's rejection. She could see that now.

"You need a life, too."

The path rejoined the sidewalk at the end of Water Street near Adriana's house. "Wow, falling in love has changed your perspective. Aren't you the introverted one who hated being around people? I'm pretty sure you didn't like others telling you to get a life."

Jasmine turned to face her, searching her eyes. "You're right. I'm sorry, but I worry about how hard you work. Can you hire some help and get more time off?"

"We're working on it." Kass sighed. "Hailey finally agreed, since we have no backup with Ava's broken leg, and the last girl we hired isn't really up to par. We need at least two more employees, so if you know anyone looking for work, please send them our way."

"I'll keep an eye out."

And she would, too. Jasmine didn't say that lightly. Meanwhile, though, Jasmine hooked her arm through Kass's and towed her up the walkway at Adriana's house. Adriana's and Myles's. It still seemed strange to think of Adriana married after having been widowed longer than Kass had known her.

Jasmine pressed the doorbell and, a moment later,

Adriana whisked the door open. "Hey! Come on in. You're just in time to do some taste testing."

The fragrance of luscious chocolate swirled out, and Kass's mouth watered.

"Sure... but I was hoping you'd have a few minutes to talk wedding dresses. I can come back another time for that, though." Jasmine sniffed the air. "Smells good."

"Oh, I've got only one more pan to run through the oven, so I've got time. Myles just put on a pot of coffee since he bumped into our new neighbor out back. Have you met Wesley Ferguson yet? They're out on the deck, so go on through, and I'll be there in a minute. Did you bring sketches or anything?"

Jasmine followed Adriana into the kitchen, but Kass hung back. Wesley was here? Mr. Gorgeous Hunk with the insecure young son who tugged at Kass's heartstrings? Both of them had that effect, but she was being silly. Even though single dads seemed to need a woman in their lives, she'd been mistaken before. Cue the music for Mason... and his twins, who'd been about Sebastian's age when she fell for their father. Avery, especially, had hero-worshiped every woman who paid her any attention. Kass had loved that little girl.

Kass wasn't sure she wanted to get to know Wesley Ferguson. Didn't want to start dreaming about him and Sebastian, and how she could complete the circle in their lives. And, besides, she didn't want her friends to start getting any ideas.

Ideas? About what? She'd rarely worried they'd get

ideas about her and Peter, or her and Basil, or her and any other man in the neighborhood. Since when was that even an issue? It wasn't.

She braced herself and followed Jasmine and Adriana out to the back deck.

CHAPTER 4

*Y*ou'll like Bridgeview Elementary." Myles handed Wesley a cup of coffee — black, as requested — and settled into a wicker chair nearby. "I've only been teaching there a year, but it's been a breath of fresh air for me."

"It had a good rep when I looked it up online." Wesley had done his homework before buying. "I was considering another property near Holmes Elementary, but proximity to the river clinched the deal here." Either would have been close enough to Sydney's parents' place. He certainly didn't want to live next door.

"We're glad to have you. And, Sebastian, you'll like Ms. Torrington. She's really nice."

Sebastian glanced up from the game he was playing on Wesley's phone. He didn't make eye contact with Myles, but nodded enough for an acknowledgment.

How much should Wesley push his son? Sydney's mother had lined up a counselor, a speech therapist, and a shrink for her only grandson. He suppressed a shudder. Sebastian would be fine once they settled in and he felt secure after life with Sydney and the trauma of her death. Wesley needed Astrid and Robert's help, but not too much. It would be a delicate balance.

The French door behind Myles swung open and a young woman with long dark hair stepped out, laughing at something someone said from inside the house.

Wesley stilled, narrowing his gaze at his host. If this was a setup...

Myles swiveled in his chair. "Hi, Jasmine! How are you doing? Have you met our new neighbor yet?"

The young woman smiled. "Sorry, I just dropped by to talk wedding dresses with Adriana if she had a minute."

Talk wedding dresses? That meant... Wesley took in the diamond on Jasmine's finger and forced himself to relax.

"Hi. I'm Jasmine Santoro. You must be Wesley. My brother Marco mentioned meeting you." She came closer and held out her hand.

Wesley rose and shook it. "Wesley Ferguson. Yes, I met Marco at church yesterday. His son is Sebastian's age."

"He has three." Jasmine chuckled. "Caden, Oren, and Arie. I'm guessing it's the middle one you mean."

"Yes, Oren. Pleased to meet you."

Adriana came out onto the deck carrying a tray. Behind her, Kassidy North closed the French door then glanced up and met Wesley's gaze before offering a tentative smile. "Hi, Wesley."

"You've met?" asked Myles.

Kassidy nodded. "At the bakery on Saturday."

At least she didn't say *how*.

Adriana set the tray on a side table and began distributing bowls of chocolate brownies topped with ice cream. "I'm impressed you remember anyone who came in with that huge crowd."

Here was her chance to tell her friends about Sebastian's clumsiness. Instead, her cheeks flushed slightly. She glanced at him then away. "It was pretty crazy in there all day. I'll tell everyone I meet... if you know anyone looking for part-time work, Hailey and I are hiring."

Jasmine scrunched up her face. "Doesn't help that my cousin broke her leg."

"Sure doesn't. But we shouldn't have let ourselves get so short-staffed that there was no one to pick up the slack. Also, we don't need another student. We need someone who can cover weekday shifts once school starts."

Adriana looked over at Wesley with a laugh. "Any experience as a waiter?"

He chuckled. "Nope, and no desire to gain any." Although... a chance to work with the pretty redhead? It might be a temptation if he had time.

"What do you do?" asked Jasmine.

"I'm a welder by trade. When Sy... when I needed more flexible hours, I started welding metal art." He shrugged. "That's what pays my bills these days." If only he could keep his galleries happy from a distance.

"Oh, that's fascinating. Kass, you should display some of his stuff at the bistro. Unless you already have a local outlet, Wesley?"

"No, just a few on the coast." Like the one in Portland that had catapulted him to some sort of fame three years ago. Sydney's accusation that he was married to his work as she flounced out the door with their son on her hip still stung. Hadn't she realized he was doing it all for her? For their future security?

Now he had Sebastian back, the boy's regressions clear in Sydney's wake. In the end, it had been a good thing Wesley wasn't tied to a nine-to-five or a certain city. His son needed him, but he also needed Sydney's parents, the only grandparents he knew.

"You should show Kass what you've got and maybe make a deal."

Wesley didn't miss the sharp glance Kassidy gave her friend before turning to him. "I'd be interested in having a look, but I should warn you, my cousin and I are looking for a certain vibe. I'm sure your style is unique and interesting, but if it doesn't match our vision for the space, I won't be able to make an offer."

"Fair enough." Wesley had seen where those rough brick walls met whitewashed planks. It didn't take an imaginative stretch to see his pieces on either back-drop. He pointed his coffee cup at the gate, still open between the two properties. "If you've got a few minutes after coffee, I could show you around this morning."

"You have plenty of time while Adriana and I talk wedding dresses," Jasmine urged.

Myles chuckled.

"Just trying to help." Jasmine shot Wesley a quick glance. "With the art, I mean."

Right. The thing was, he didn't mind showing Kassidy around. He already knew her sense of style — decor, culinary, attire — and liked it. Liked *her*, not that it mattered. If he'd been married to his work years back, it was even more true now.

"Th-thank you," whispered Sebastian as he set his empty bowl on the table beside Adriana. "G-good."

"I'm glad you enjoyed it." Adriana smiled at his son.

Maybe Wesley could relax a little and trust he'd made the right move. Good neighbors like the Sheridans weren't a given. He straightened. Where had that wild little girl gone? And why did her parents not seem to notice she was missing?

⌒⸒⸒

JASMINE AND ADRIANA bent over wedding gown photos on the patio table, talking in low tones.

Kass shouldn't have come. She'd thought it might

be fun to dream a little with her friend. After all, she was genuinely happy for Jasmine... wasn't she? But the visit wasn't shaping up the way she'd envisioned. She hadn't expected Wesley to be sitting nearby, chatting with Myles about the upcoming school year. Distracting her.

Which was all kinds of ridiculous, since she didn't know him and wasn't on the manhunt. Not that he didn't have sparkling blue eyes and gorgeous dark blond hair with a bit of wave. It *was* wavy, wasn't it? She glanced over to double-check and caught his gaze on her. Her cheeks warmed.

No more peeking.

A scrape of metal chair legs on the wooden deck dragged her gaze over again. Wesley set his bowl on the tray by Adriana. "Thanks so much. That was great and totally unexpected."

"You're welcome." Adriana straightened and smiled back. "Any time."

Wesley's gaze snagged Kass's. Again. "If you were serious about having a look, come on over."

"Um, sure. Give me a holler when you're ready to go, Jasmine."

Her friends glanced at each other with gleaming eyes. Oh, great. Jasmine fluttered her fingers. "Will do. Take your time. I'll be a while."

Sebastian ran down the steps and scooped a small gray cat into his arms. "L-Look, Daddy. I found T-Taz."

"Good job, buddy." Wesley smiled at Kass as she

came up beside him on the grassy backyard. "Short of locking the cat up in the house, I'm not sure how to keep him home. This might be a regular occurrence."

"I've never had a cat. My dad had allergies."

"Too bad." He looked pensive for a second then shook his head. "Anyway, I bought the Davenport place. It had been empty for a couple of years, from what I gather. You may have known the previous owners?"

Kass shook her head. "Not really. I've lived here less than four years, and the old man was already reclusive by then. After he passed away, it took his family a long time to clear the property and list it." She chuckled. "Hailey and I did come to the estate sale out of curiosity and picked up a few pieces of china for the bistro."

He led the way to the open gate, beckoned her through, and then closed it behind them. "Not the plate Sebastian broke, I hope."

"No. That one was from my grandmother's collection."

He turned to face her, only an inch or two taller. "Look, I'm sorry—"

"We've covered that. It's okay. It was a plate, not a life." Much as she'd love to place all the blame on his child, it truly was her own fault.

"I, uh..." Something flickered across his face. Something other than regret. Then he took her arm and steered her away from the house and toward the workshop nearer the river. He pushed open the door. "This is where the magic happens."

Shelves loaded with bins of rusty metal lined two walls. A sturdy workbench anchored the center, along with a few mammoth tools she didn't recognize. Her gaze landed on a man-sized dinosaur made of scavenged gears and machine parts. Not really her style, but impressive nonetheless. It had taken skill and imagination to weld — was that the word he'd used? — the pieces together into something so whimsical yet recognizable.

Kass reached out to touch it but pulled back before she did. "That's amazing."

"Thanks." He flashed a grin at her. "Sebastian wants to keep this one, but it's already sold. Just need to finish its partner before shipping them both."

"Oh?" Kass's eyebrows rose. "Where to?"

"A museum in Colorado." He said it so casually, as though it was an everyday occurrence.

She took a closer look around the workshop, only then spotting a group of scrap metal objects on the table. Maybe the arrangement wasn't so random, after all. Not when it looked suspiciously owl-shaped from this angle. Now, something more two-dimensional like that, mounted on the wall or perched on a high shelf, might work in the bistro.

"This steampunk owl is for a customer in Tillamook. I think I have the parts needed to finish it up, but I haven't come across them since we moved in." Wesley gestured to the shelves of bins. "They're in there some-where. Pretty sure."

Kass chewed on her lower lip as she turned to face him. "Are you really looking for a local gallery? Sounds like you keep busy with existing customers."

He had the grace to look abashed. "I'm not desperate for it, true. But I have a few unsold pieces — smaller ones — that might do well here. Only if you were serious about it, though. I can keep an eye out for another venue, so don't worry if this isn't your thing. It isn't everyone's."

"It's great. I can envision it in the bistro." That wasn't the problem. The problem was being drawn to Wesley. Mixing a business agreement with attraction seemed like a bad idea, especially since he probably had someone in his life or would have soon, and then Kass would be stuck seeing him in a business capacity.

"Great! Things are a bit crazy right now," Wesley went on. "We aren't settled in yet, but when Sebastian is in school, I'll bring a few pieces by the bistro and show you what I have in mind. What day of the week is best?"

Kass laughed. "Not Saturdays, as you noticed. Not that we have a big party every weekend, but it does tend to be our busiest day. One-thirty or two on a weekday is good, after the lunch rush but before the old men stake out their usual tables for coffee and checkers."

"Sounds go—"

"Oh, except I'm not there every Wednesday. Sometimes I have cooking club at the community center."

"The once-a-month thing I saw advertised?"

She shot him a look. He'd noticed? It did sound like the perfect thing for a single dad. Which sent her mind back to Galena Landing and Mason Waterman. She'd worked with him to prep meals ahead, and then he'd gone and married someone else. Well, here in Bridgeview she ran the classes for the community, not with finding her own partner in mind. There was no reason Wesley couldn't attend, if he wanted. Several men did.

The project was more a service than a money-maker, a way to make a difference in people's lives in a more personal way than selling them sourdough bread and cinnamon rolls.

"I grabbed a pamphlet on Saturday and meant to look up the website and join. I'm not that great a cook, day in and day out."

Kass shook her thoughts away. "Having a stash in the freezer really helps. I keep some meals on hand, too, even though Hailey and I often have leftovers from the bistro. I really hate dragging myself up the stairs to the apartment, not knowing what's for dinner after a long day on my feet."

"I know what you mean."

Her gaze caught on his. She really shouldn't be thinking any kinds of thoughts about this man. She didn't know him. Didn't know why he appeared to be raising a child on his own. "Been on your own long?" A flush swooped up her cheeks. Why on earth had that come out of her mouth?

He held her gaze. "Sebastian's mother died a while back."

"I, I'm sorry. It's none of my business." And it definitely shouldn't make her happy.

"It's a long story, Kassidy, but—"

"Kass. My friends call me Kass." What, now she was inviting him to friendship? Had her mouth lost all connection with her brain?

Wesley tipped his head. "Kass."

"You were about to say...?"

He shook his head. "Never mind. It isn't important. Not right now, anyway. The only pertinent bit is that there is no woman in our lives. You? Are you seeing someone?"

Her mouth opened and closed. Was he asking what she thought he was asking? As though it mattered to him if she were doing life solo or not? "I, uh, there's no one."

"Good to know." His eyes glimmered and a tiny smile poked at his cheeks under his trim beard as he ushered her into the sunny backyard.

It seemed much warmer than it had ten minutes ago. "I should be going. Jasmine is likely done with Adriana, and we've planned a couple of hours out on the river."

He quirked an eyebrow. "Swimming? Rafting?"

Kass hesitated. Admitting she fished to a city guy she'd just met seemed like a bad idea. Sure, he'd bought a place along the river, but he needed a large yard for his business. He couldn't probably weld freely with close neighbors on all sides. It was likely noisy. "I love being on the water. Nature relaxes me."

He grinned. "Me, too."

A step in the right direction, but what did it matter, even if he wondered if she was dating or not? He needed friends like Adriana and Myles and Daria and Marco. People with kids. People who weren't her. "Anyway, I'll see you when you come by the bistro."

He fell into step beside her as they walked toward the gate. Sebastian leaned over a board laid over sawhorses beside a trash can, picking up a small object that gleamed in the sunshine. Gold?

Her steps faltered as Saturday's conversation flowed over her. The broken plate. Wesley's offer to... what, fix it? She'd brushed the words aside, since the offer was completely meaningless in the light of the shattered porcelain.

Kass veered toward the little boy, aware of Wesley catching his breath beside her. She didn't let that deter her. "Hey, Sebastian. What are you doing?" She kept her voice light, friendly.

The boy froze, the golden filigree ear of her prized plate clutched in his hand. He glanced between her and his father and dropped the piece. It clattered onto the makeshift table.

Kass's hands found her hips as she whirled to face Wesley. Her elbow caught his ribs, and her eyebrows shot up.

He backed up a step, both hands in the air. "It was out with the trash."

"That didn't make it yours to take."

"It was out with the *trash*," he repeated more slowly. "By definition, trash is unwanted. Why not keep it out of the landfill? Make something beautiful out of it?"

"Because..." She couldn't answer. There was nothing to say. But beautiful? It was in at least a dozen pieces. Even arranged on the board in a semblance of its former shape, it was nothing but a pile of broken, worthless china. Why should it bother her if he had it in his possession? He was right. She'd tossed it, expecting waste management to haul it away... hopefully before Hailey saw it.

Kass shook her head and headed for the gate to Adriana's backyard. The unwelcome discovery was no more unsettling than Wesley himself.

CHAPTER 5

*H*ow are things going?" Astrid set a tray of teacups on the balcony table between Wesley and Robert then helped herself. She settled into a wrought-iron chair across from them.

Wesley didn't even need to ask what was in the cups. With Astrid, it was always green tea. She'd read about the benefits somewhere and decreed it perfect. A minimalist like her only needed one kind of hot beverage in her cupboards.

Living in the same city and drinking tea that tasted like grass was the price he paid for having uncontested custody of Sebastian. At least on *his* watch his son got the comfort of a more normal life. Weren't hot dogs, French fries, and pop requirements for a growing child?

"We're getting settled in. It takes time, partly because I have orders to fill that can't wait, and when I've caught up for the day, I like to spend the time exploring with Sebastian. It's nice to be able to use our bikes to get around the neighborhood."

"I'm still concerned about the river flowing by the back of your property. That just doesn't seem safe with a young child."

The river was all that made city living remotely bearable. Once Sebastian was asleep, Wesley could step out to the backyard and relax in nature — listening to the coyotes, inhaling the scent of the cottonwoods, gazing at the stars, and flicking a line in the water — all the while keeping his back door in view.

"Drop it, Astrid." Robert narrowed his gaze at his wife. "He already bought it."

"There's a fence across the back. Sebastian knows he's not to go through the gate. When I get a minute, I'll raise the latch so he can't reach, but I'm not really worried about it. He's cautious, and my workshop is right there. It's an ideal setup, really." Huh, he could raise the latch on the side gate, too. Might not be a bad idea, all things considered... like Violet.

Astrid opened her mouth to reply but glanced at Robert, pursed her lips, and raised her teacup.

Wesley reached for the one nearest his elbow. He took a gulp of the hot liquid. Didn't matter what it smelled like, he had to drink it to be polite. The stuff nearly gagged him. It tasted worse than dirt. And who drank scalding tea on a hot summer evening, anyway? Only Astrid.

"Bridgeview is a great community, and very safe. It's

down in the valley with few through-streets, and even the bridge to the north shore shoots overhead. It reminds me of one town I lived in, years ago, where kids played in the streets, and no one thought anything of it. The neighbors kept an eye out and sent the kids home at sundown from wherever they were." That placement was one small bright spot in his fractured childhood.

Astrid scowled at him. "The world isn't that secure anymore."

Robert cleared his throat. "Coddling the boy won't do any good, either." They glared at each other.

Sydney'd said her parents' bickering drove her out as a teen, and she'd rarely been back, even after Sebastian had been born. Thankfully they lived in an over-fifty building, or Astrid would have insisted they combine households.

Wesley hadn't had the opportunity to demonstrate his love for his son for much of the boy's life. He was going to make up for it now. He'd be both parents, which was two more than he'd had. He'd provide security and freedom, and Sebastian would thrive. He'd show Astrid and Robert that he was far more than the workaholic unwanted loser Sydney had fled.

"It's not too late to enroll Sebastian in the alternative school here. I know bussing isn't an option from your side of the river, but I have time. I could drive him."

Wesley took a deep breath. Astrid was like a dog

with a bone. Would she ever stop questioning decisions he'd already made? "Bridgeview Elementary is great. In fact, we live next door to the second grade teacher, and he's answered many of my questions. Did you know the PTA raised money and got grants for a greenhouse, and all the classes have a gardening component?" That ought to appease Astrid. "Myles says parents are very involved, and the kids love it."

"Will you have time to be involved? Or are you too busy making..." She waved a hand in an elaborate design. "...art?"

"I'll make time. You keep forgetting that my son is everything to me." He smiled at her to soften the words. "I met a guy who has three sons, one of whom is Sebastian's age. Marco teaches jiu-jitsu at the community center, and I'm thinking of signing Sebastian up for that. It starts in mid-September."

"Martial arts?" Astrid set her teacup down a little too hard. "But non-violence—"

"Astrid."

"But..."

Robert shook his head.

Wesley leaned forward. "It's more about instilling confidence than about fighting. Sure, he'll learn some moves, but the idea is to teach him to avoid conflict in the first place. Myles — my next-door neighbor — says that bullying has dropped significantly at Bridgeview Elementary since they began encouraging kids to enroll in jiu-jitsu. His stepson was picked on a lot when he was younger, but he learned to stand up for himself, and the situation improved."

"Because of fighting."

"No, Astrid, because Sam stopped seeing himself as a victim." Wesley glanced over his shoulder into the living room, where Sebastian played a video game with headphones on. Probably a good thing Astrid couldn't see the screen. "With Sebastian's shyness and stuttering, I don't want him to be an easy mark. I want him to be confident in who he is."

"Good goals." Robert nodded.

"Well, yes, but..." Astrid raised both hands in surrender. "I guess I don't have to like it."

Wesley smiled. He wasn't going to take that bait. Maybe he wouldn't have to remind Astrid constantly of the ground rules they'd agreed upon. Robert seemed willing to do it for him.

"Are you seeing anyone?" Astrid asked a little too brightly.

"We moved in two weeks ago."

"I just wondered..." She glanced at Robert, who leaned back and closed his eyes.

Hopefully that didn't mean this was a conversation Sydney's father would stay out of. Wesley shrugged. "I'm not looking, but I'm not ruling it out, either." A certain redhead drifted through his mind. As if she'd take on someone like him. Laughable. "I've got other things to focus on. Getting settled, meeting neighbors, fixing up the house, and, oh yeah—" he snapped his fingers "—filling orders. Not much time to hang out at the singles bar."

"There are other places."

"We went to church." Now, why had he said that?

"Oh, please, Wesley. Don't even start Sebastian on that gobbledygook."

"Astrid."

Thanks, Robert. Maybe.

Sydney's dad took a sip of tea and even seemed to enjoy it. "A little religion never hurt anyone."

"That's not true. Remember—"

Wesley shot to his feet. "Astrid, we had a deal. I'd live here with Sebastian so you could have all the access to him that you want. Your part is not interfering. Being grand-parents, not life advisors." He didn't dare say everything he wanted. How heavy was the threat they'd take Sebastian from him? Robert was an attorney. Not family law, but no doubt he had friends. The biggest buffer was that Astrid would have to give up her lifestyle and the condo. For them to fight for custody would be a big decision.

"I only think—"

"My part is providing a home for my son. Meeting his needs. That's more than food and clothes, no matter what Sydney told you I was capable of. Yes, I've drifted a lot, but I had no reason not to after Sydney left. Now I have all the reason in the world. Sebastian needs me, but he also needs to be part of a community, and I've found one in Bridgeview."

"But... church?"

"Church. School. Jiu-jitsu." He eyed her. "Our new life together."

Robert nodded and leaned back. "We did agree."

Astrid's lips tightened into a line. Finally she sighed. "You drive a hard bargain."

"It was already driven. Now let's keep it in mind, shall we?" He flexed his fingers, shaking out the fists that had formed without his awareness. "It's time for me to get Sebastian home. He's been playing that game long enough."

Astrid opened her mouth then obviously thought better of speaking.

"It's not like there's anything for him to do here." Wesley pointed across the strip of green to the townhouses next door. "There aren't any kids, and the playground is blocks away." He'd need to invite the Jansens to his riverside home oftener than coming here. Only, would Astrid know when to go home?

$\sim$

KASS READ the classified ad over one more time before clicking *send payment*. She let out a long sigh as she snapped her laptop shut and set it aside. "I really hate running an ad like that. Who knows what kind of person will decide to show up for an interview?"

Her cousin looked up from filing her nails. "Only

ones we invite. I'm more worried no one will want a job, and we'll be stuck limping along."

"Yeah, there are plenty of students looking, but I purposefully said daytimes."

"Maybe a mom whose kids are all in school for the first time, who wants to pick up a bit of spending money."

"One can hope." Kass leaned back in the comfy sofa in their upstairs apartment. "It's so crazy busy. I need a vacation or something." Was it the pace in the bistro that caused her restlessness, or something more? She'd been unsettled ever since she'd met Wesley and his adorable-but-needy little boy.

Hailey's eyebrows flickered, but she didn't look up. Instead, she reached for a bottle of vibrant turquoise nail polish from the side table.

Kass pressed her point. "We don't even have time to get professional manicures." Her own pink nails needed to be stripped and redone, but she couldn't summon the energy.

"Book off a spa day."

As if that would be the best way for Kass to relax, unlike her cousin. "We don't have enough employees to cover that. Ava won't be back until September." And by then Kass would officially have gone crazy.

"You put an ad in the Spokesman-Review. Plus we have a Help Wanted sign in the window. We'll get staff."

"And then we'll have to train them."

Hailey drew the brush down one long nail, leaving a glistening turquoise trail in its wake. "Comes with the territory of owning a business. We should be glad we're doing so well only three years in."

"I know." Kass *did* know. But, while she and Hailey had always been able to talk about nearly everything, she shied away from discussing the restlessness inside her. Hailey would either freak out and send her for counseling or laugh it off. It wasn't like Kass could explain. She loved the bakery and bistro. She did. Even working with Hailey every day was fine.

But... did she want to do this until she was old and gray? Because, right now, it felt like they were frozen in time. She and her cousin would still be sitting here at forty, fifty, sixty, both crotchety, both single. Sure, Hailey never missed a chance to notice a new man on the horizon. She flirted like crazy, but she never seemed to settle on one and pursue him.

Kass couldn't even bring herself to flirt. Not after she'd all but thrown herself at Mason Waterman back in Galena Landing and been brushed aside. She let out a long sigh.

Hailey glanced up. "Seriously. Book a massage, a pedicure, something. If we need to open late one morning, it won't be the end of the world."

"I can't. But thank you." Kass stared as her cousin finished painting her nails, screwed the top back on the bottle, and set it aside.

"You've been out of sorts lately." Hailey raised her eyebrows.

She'd been trying to hide it. Obviously unsuccessfully. "Nothing a few more employees won't cure." And a week in nature by herself.

"Maybe you should cancel that once-a-month cooking club thing."

"No."

Hailey shrugged. "It eats up a lot of your time."

"Only a couple of afternoons a month."

"Plus menu-planning and shopping."

"True, but it's worthwhile helping people."

Her phone dinged with an incoming email. Kass thumbed it open to find a notification from her webform of a new signup to the cooking club. Good timing. She held up the phone. "The program makes a big difference in people's lives. I just had someone new join." She scrolled down to scan the information. Wait. Wesley Ferguson? Was that a good thing, or a not-so-good thing? Why had he even landed on her radar to start with? Whatever she needed in her life, it wasn't another single father who gave off bad-boy vibes. Hadn't she learned anything from Mason?

"Anyone we know?" Hailey drummed a staccato beat on the end table, drying her nails.

"The new guy who lives by Adriana."

Her cousin made a face. "The hot one with the kid."

Sounded about right. Not that Kass would use

those words or acknowledge them to Hailey. She pretended to read from the screen. "Wesley Ferguson."

"We need some new men in Bridgeview with less baggage." Hailey sighed, pursing her lips.

Kass let out a bitter chuckle as she set her phone down. "I hate to break it to you, but we're on the downhill slide to thirty. There aren't many men our age who aren't on the rebound from something or other."

"I don't see you settling."

Her cousin also couldn't see how many times Wesley strolled through her head. "How about you? You're a year older."

"Don't remind me."

"If I didn't know better, I'd think you'd already been wounded in love."

Hailey bounced to her feet. "Maybe I have. Want a pop?"

"No, thanks. I want to hear more about this great, secret trial in your life."

"Ha ha." Hailey crossed the open living area and tugged open the fridge. "You sure? There's root beer, cola, ginger ale..."

"I know what there is." Kass followed Hailey and leaned on the island. "Talk."

Her cousin pulled the tab on a ginger ale and lifted the fizzy drink in salute. "In your dreams." She sauntered down the short hallway and into her bedroom.

Kass glanced at the clock. Since when did Hailey seclude herself at nine o'clock? She was the night owl between them. Since she didn't want to talk, apparently. And that was downright interesting, since there'd never been a hint of any real romance in Hailey's life that Kass knew of. Sure, they'd lived together for less than four years, but they'd been close all their lives. How had Kass missed this?

Better to mull over Hailey's situation than over her own. Because Wesley Ferguson needed to be banished from her brain.

CHAPTER 6

*S*ebastian tightened his grip around Wesley's hand as they approached the community center. "I d-don't want to."

"It'll be fine, buddy. Oren will be here, and some other kids."

"V-Violet?"

"Nope." Adriana had even offered to watch Sebastian, but that was a big *no-way* considering, well, Violet. Thankfully, she'd also assured him that a few other men attended when Wesley had panicked he'd be surrounded by women.

Wesley pulled open the heavy wooden doors and choked back a whistle. This red-brick building had obviously been built in a similar era to Bridgeview Bakery and Bistro.

A middle-aged woman looked up from building a tower with a toddler on a large mat near the front window. "Hi there! I'm Winnie Santoro. You must be Wesley and Sebastian."

Sebastian sidled behind Wesley.

"That's us. We're here for the cooking club?"

"They're just getting started back in the kitchen. Sebastian, I have some puzzles and books along for big kids like you. Want to see?"

Sebastian shook his head against Wesley's hip.

Wesley knelt. "You sure, buddy? Daddy's going to be busy getting food ready."

"Can I w-watch?"

"I'm sure he can," Winnie said warmly. "I can't imagine he'll get in the way. If you change your mind, little man, come on out here any time. Okay?"

"Thanks." Wesley offered the woman a smile then turned to the open doorway at the back of the space, where a cacophony of female voices greeted him.

But what was this on the wall? A large white box, rather thin, marked Tesla.

A woman he'd seen at church stood in the kitchen doorway. "Admiring our Powerwall?"

"A what? It looks very... techy."

She laughed. "It is. It's a storage battery. This whole community center runs off solar. I'm Eden Riehl, by the way. My husband is the solar architect who installed it."

"Wesley Ferguson and my son, Sebastian." His fingers skimmed the glossy white trim as his mind buzzed with possibilities. "I'd love to hear more about it."

"Jacob would be happy to talk, trust me. You bought the old Davenport place by Adriana's, didn't you? Lots of trees on that property."

"Yes, that's the place and, you're right, it's probably too shaded. But I'm still curious."

"I'll let Jacob know. Usually it's him coming to the cooking club, not me, but he's out of town on a work project for a few days, so I took the afternoon off to fill our freezer for the next few weeks. Once you're accustomed to having meals at the ready, it's hard to imagine not having them for a month."

"I bet. I've never done this, but I'm looking forward to knowing what's for dinner."

Eden stepped back, beckoning. "Come on in. Sorry for distracting you."

"No apology needed. I'd already stopped to look." He followed her into the bustling kitchen lined with stainless counters and backsplashes. Several ranges and wall ovens marched down the end wall. A humungous island, also covered with stainless, anchored the center. Half a dozen women surrounded it, chatting while they arranged supplies.

Kass North stood at the end, her red hair pulled back into a ponytail. Her gaze lifted to meet his.

He was vaguely aware of Eden introducing him and reciting names of the others, but he'd never retain them anyway. Kass's name he remembered, along with her pretty brown eyes and her warm smile. Yes, he'd been fully aware she taught this class, but that still hadn't prepared him for seeing her in this setting.

"Hi, Wesley."

"Hi." Where was Mr. Suave when Wesley needed him? Vanished.

"I see you brought a helper today. Why don't the two of you find a spot somewhere? We're nearly ready to start." She consulted a clipboard. "We're expecting a couple of more people."

Wesley cupped his hand around Sebastian's head and pointed him at the island, where two women scooted to either side, making room.

"Well, aren't you a cutie?" A woman in a tight, low-cut tank leaned toward Sebastian. "Sure look like your daddy, don't you?" She winked at Wesley.

The woman was a train wreck waiting to happen. He shifted slightly, angling away from her, both hands on Sebastian's shoulders. When he looked up, he caught Kass's gaze as she frowned slightly at the forward woman. So, either this was typical behavior, or it wasn't. Either way, it bugged Kass, and that made his heart inexplicably happy.

"I'm Catalina Romero. Single mom. Three kids." The woman pressed against Wesley's arm. "Available."

"Can I have everyone's attention, please? Our late-comers will just have to catch up when they arrive." Kass skewered Catalina with a sour look. "You should all have received the menu in your inbox a couple of days ago, so you know what we'll be cooking up today. Eden, can I get you at the first station, sautéing ground beef? Catalina, I've got you on chopping onions. Trudy, please start packaging the spices for the pork rub." She glanced at the door. "Ah, there you are, Peter. You're on salad dressings."

Wesley turned around. Whew, another man, and one he'd seen at church last week.

The guy grinned at him with a nod, slipping into the spot Catalina vacated. "Sorry I'm late, Kass."

She laughed. "I'd hate for you to get the dregs job."

Hadn't she already given that to the hussy? Wesley shifted from one foot to the other, catching the warmth in Kass's eyes as she looked at Peter. Were they an item? That'd be just his luck. She'd said there wasn't anyone special in her life, but maybe she wished there were. He gave his head a quick shake as she raised her eyebrows at him. Oops, what did she think he meant?

"Wesley, can I put you and Sebastian on garlic bread? Everything is set up over beside the pantry door." She pointed behind him.

He saluted. "You've got it." The participants drifted to their stations, seeming to know what they were doing. He turned to see a stack of French loaves with a sticky note on the cupboard door above it. Directions, hopefully. "Come on, buddy. Let's figure this thing out."

THE BOUQUET OF COOKING BEEF, simmering tomato sauce, and pungent pesto combined into an overwhelming flood of smells, but Kass was used to it. As everyone began chopping, measuring, or mixing, she made her way across the busy space to where Wesley fumbled with peeling the skins off the garlic cloves she'd left him.

"Need a tip?"

He looked up. "Please."

She leaned past him for a large butcher knife and heard his breath catch. *Don't be like Catalina,* she warned herself. "Sorry about that." She set out a full head of garlic then laid the knife across it, flat-bladed. One quick push and the head broke into cloves. She cleared most of them out of the way then repeated the process several times with single cloves.

"Sebastian, your job is to pick the peels off them once your dad crushes them. Like this." She handed one clove to the boy then popped the skin off another one. "The peels go in here, and the garlic in here. Okay?"

The boy nodded. When he'd separated the garlic from the skin, he flashed her a quick grin.

Whew. She didn't usually allow kids to remain in the kitchen, but something told her if she didn't, Wesley would simply ask for a refund and be gone. A single dad new to town with a super-shy kid... she got it. Soon enough the boy would be comfortable with

Winnie if he wasn't at school during the cooking session.

Wesley's fingers brushed hers as he took the knife from her hand. She heard her own breath intake sharply as her gaze flew to meet his. He was so close. No, it was her. She was in his space, but backing up out of it was difficult, almost painful, with their eyes focused on each other.

"I, um, I'll get the food processor. I should have set it up here to start with. You'll want it for mixing the garlic, butter, salt, and herbs." She took another step back.

"Thanks."

It only bought her a minute before she returned with the appliance and plugged it into the backsplash. "If you need a hand with anything else, let me know."

He'd already crushed a few more cloves while Sebastian separated out the papery skins. He glanced at her. "How long have you been doing this?"

"The cooking club?" Kass looked around, but everyone seemed busy with their assigned tasks. "Since January. I mean, officially. A few friends and I used to get together to meal prep before that."

"It's a great space for it."

"It is. The community worked hard to renovate the building, add this state-of-the-art kitchen, switch everything to solar. We've been using it for less than a year now."

"I saw the Powerwall."

She grinned. "Isn't it great? If Hailey and I hadn't just done a complete renovation of our building, we'd be sorely tempted to go solar there. But we'd already spent a ton of money on the electrical systems."

"Still, running this program must take a lot of time away from the bistro."

"That's what Hailey says, but I feel like it's just as needed." Kass grimaced. "Not everyone has the budget to eat meals out or the skills or time to keep on top of cooking. I like organizing the menus by the season. About half the meals this time are planned for the grill, but next month we'll be switching over to the fall menu with more slow-cooker meals."

"Must be even harder to source if you switch menus seasonally." Wesley shot her an admiring look.

Kass flushed. "Well, yes, but we really believe in fresh ingredients and source them locally whenever we can. You met Jasmine the other day. She and her cousin Peter — over there mixing ranch dressing — started Bridgeview Backyards this year, where they're growing produce and selling it by subscription and at the farmers market. They had a third partner..." No, a complete stranger wouldn't hear about Basil Santoro's DUI and current time in jail from her. That was just plain gossip, even though it was true. "Anyway, they hope to expand over the next two or three years but, meanwhile, I've been able to take some excess tomatoes and green beans off their hands." She thumbed over her shoulder to where the pastor's wife, Juanita Ramirez, sliced the ends off a mountain of green beans.

Wesley pressed the side of his blade over another head of garlic. "A woman of many talents."

She shook her head. "Me? No. I just love food, and I love my community. That's all."

His gaze met hers once again. "I think there's more to you than that, Kassidy North."

"Kass? Where do you want this pile of onions?" Catalina's strident voice came from across the kitchen.

Kass pivoted away from Wesley. She should be paying attention. No one should have to hunt her down to find out their next step. She couldn't let a good-looking man with intense blue eyes distract her from the job she was supposed to be doing.

Only... what had he been about to say?

CHAPTER 7

*W*esley stacked the full containers into his cardboard box. Initial membership into the cooking club had seemed a little steep until he realized he was buying reusable containers with airtight lids. While he loved prowling around landfills more than most people — he'd discovered a lot of good junk for his metal sculptures there, after all — he also appreciated conservation where possible.

He glanced around the community kitchen. Nearly everyone had left, many towing stacked rolling coolers behind them. They must live nearer the community center than he did, because the thought of hauling coolers down the long set of stairs beneath the bridge or several extra blocks around on steep streets made no sense. He'd brought the truck.

Sebastian nudged him. "C-can we have garlic t-toast tonight?"

"He sure has a lot of trouble talking for such a big kid." Catalina stood mere inches away, frowning at Sebastian. "How old are you? Seven? Eight?"

It was her business how? Wesley touched his son's shoulder. "Six, actually."

"I think you should—"

Wesley sliced his hand through the air. "I think you shouldn't give me advice. I'm handling things, okay?"

She rolled her eyes. "No need to be touchy. I know how hard it is raising kids alone. I was just trying to help."

He forced a smile. "No need." So much for hanging around a few extra minutes and talking to Kass again. It was time to get out of here. He hefted the box and headed for the street. A moment later he'd slammed the Tundra's tailgate and turned to open the backdoor, but no little boy was there, ready to clamber in.

Hadn't his son been right behind him? "Sebastian?" He whirled.

Kass crouched on the community center steps, one hand on Sebastian's small shoulder. His shy son smiled at something she said, and she grinned back. After two hours in the kitchen, her ponytail had loosened a little, and tendrils of reddish hair framed her face. She was so pretty in a pair of long jean shorts and a mint-colored sleeveless blouse.

Wesley stilled.

Was he really thinking of dating? Allowing a woman into their life? Not just any woman. Kassidy North.

Even though he'd entertained the thought for several days, he'd pushed the dreams aside. Sebastian was at a vulnerable stage. He'd lost his mother only six months ago, after all.

Kass tipped her head back and laughed at something his son had said, and Sebastian giggled.

Giggled.

When had that last happened? No amount of dredging into the recent past brought a memory.

She ruffled Sebastian's short hair and stood, only then noticing Wesley watching them. She smiled, the skin around her brown eyes crinkling, a little dimple creasing her left cheek.

Wesley felt like a teenager as a goofy grin crossed his face. Not that his teens were a pleasant memory with being shuffled from one foster home to another. He'd had no aptitude for school, but plenty for trouble. Thankfully one placement had been in the home of the high school shop teacher. Too bad it had ended with the teacher's divorce... Wesley had thrived on the woodworking and mechanics classes.

Kass looked like a Math and English kind of woman. The kind who'd been on honor roll and maybe valedictorian. The kind who wouldn't have given him a second look back then. Not many girls had.

High school was a long way back, though. Now he knew who he was and had honed his strengths. He knew what he wanted, and that was a chance with

Kassidy North. If only he could get his tongue untied and ask.

"You've got a good kid here." Kass nudged Sebastian forward. "He was a terrific helper in the kitchen today. And, since he likes cinnamon more than chocolate, I promised him a cinnamon cookie next time you pop into the bakery."

"Cinnamon?" Great, he sounded like a dolt.

Sebastian nodded eagerly, eyes shining. "C-can we, Dad? Now?"

"Don't we have enough food?" Wesley gestured at the box in the pickup bed. "There's even a couple of cakes in there."

Kass chuckled. "But no cinnamon cookies." She met his gaze. "Up to you, of course. You're the boss."

He took a deep breath. "Tell you what. If you don't have plans for this evening, how about we go for a picnic, and you can bring dessert? Cinnamon cookies sound amazing." Wait. Had he really asked her out?

She stared at him, her mouth frozen slightly open.

He stared back, probably about the same, but she hadn't turned him down. Yet. "I know you're used to gourmet everything, but I'm a pretty basic guy. Fried chicken takeout?"

This was crazy. A man planning a first date should actually plan, not mumble apologetically about takeout. Why didn't she say anything?

Sebastian spun around, pumping his fist. "Yes!"

Somehow, that broke the spell. Smiling, Kass glanced down at his son then met Wesley's gaze. "I can't tonight, but maybe tomorrow? We close the bistro at five."

"Five o'clock tomorrow? Sure. That'd be terrific." She'd really agreed? "I might be able to come up with something better than takeout." Maybe. If he spent all afternoon in the kitchen, but he didn't have time for that.

She lifted her pretty shoulder in a slight shrug as she smiled. "It doesn't matter. If you don't have anywhere else in mind, we could go out to the Bowl and Pitcher. It's a nice wild spot along the river with picnic tables."

"Sounds great. I can pick you up at the bistro or at your place, whichever you prefer."

Kass let out a small laugh. "My cousin and I live upstairs in the same building, so out front about five-thirty would be great. That gives me a few minutes to get ready."

He hadn't even thought of her living there, but it made sense. Although he was accustomed to living and working from the same location, he'd go stir crazy in an apartment. Hadn't Kass told him how much she loved nature?

⌒ℓℓ

HAILEY CLOSED her copy of People magazine and laid

it on the coffee table as she looked up. "Didn't everyone help with cleanup today?"

Kass glanced at the clock. Oops. She was later than usual. She set her purse on the closet shelf and kicked off her sandals. "Yes, we got out of the community center on time. Want a pop or iced tea?" She angled into the apartment kitchen and opened the fridge.

"Ginger ale, while you're up. Thanks."

"Sure." Kass poured herself an iced tea, grabbed a can of pop for her cousin, and turned back to the living room. It wasn't a question of whether she was ready to talk about Wesley with Hailey. She'd agreed to go out with him tomorrow, so it was time to open up.

"How come you're late getting home? I brought a container of gazpacho up for supper, by the way."

"Perfect." Kass collapsed into her favorite chair and propped her feet on the ottoman. "I'm going out to the Bowl and Pitcher tomorrow after work."

Hailey made a face. "Now if you were going someplace with a beach, I'd be all over it. How about Liberty Lake? I haven't been swimming much this summer."

"Um... I'm not inviting you. I'm going with Wesley."

"A date?" Hailey set the can down, leaned forward, and clasped her hands together, giving Kass her undivided attention. "With Wesley? The hot guy with..."

"With the little boy. Yes."

"There are other guys. Ones without kids."

Kass took a long drink of her iced tea.

"Kass, seriously. You seem to have this thing for

men with kids. Why? Marry some guy without all the baggage and have children of your own. You don't want to be a stepmother. Don't want to be compared to the other woman, whether she was good or bad."

"Are you done?"

"Only if I've convinced you."

"You haven't." Not that the question was inappropriate, exactly. She'd wondered the same thing herself, back when she was interested in Mason. That was a situation where she hadn't worried about the children's mother, especially not once she'd met the loser that was Erin. No, it had been Liz Nemesek, ghost of Mason's past, she'd needed to be concerned with, something she hadn't realized until she'd been more than halfway in love with Mason.

Wesley had said Sebastian's mom was dead, so that ruled out a repeat performance of Erin showing up with all her belongings in tow. But when had it happened? Had he and Sydney been happily married? Kass needed answers before she could fall in love.

"Stepmothers have a bad rap for a reason."

"Hailey, here's what you can do. Pray for me. Listen. Give me advice when I ask for it. But please don't judge."

Her cousin flopped back on the sofa like the prima donna she was, rolling her eyes. "Sure. Whatever."

"I'm serious. Don't get all bossy with me when you won't even tell me why you flirt with every guy with a whiff of testosterone. You talk big, but you've got no follow-through."

"I'll get us each a bowl of gazpacho. Plus, there were some sourdough biscuits left today, so I'll reheat those." Hailey surged to her feet.

"Like that," hollered Kass. "Queen of changing the subject." Why hadn't she ever noticed before? Hadn't they talked about nearly everything as teens and young adults, and even more so in the several years they'd lived and worked together?

Keyword: *nearly* everything. Maybe Hailey's subject changes had been more subtle in years gone by. So subtle Kass hadn't even noticed. Still, it seemed there must have been bits of dropped information she should have picked up on and added together. She'd be on the watch now.

Out of sight in the kitchen, the microwave hummed. Dishes clanked. The tap turned on and off.

Kass wandered into the kitchen. "Oh, Daria mentioned that Basil's doing his jail time starting Monday."

Her cousin didn't turn from the sink.

"Thirty days. He's lucky he didn't get more than that, but I guess they're more lenient on a first DUI offense." It had been a couple of months since Jasmine's brother had tried to run a police barricade while under the influence.

Hailey ladled gazpacho into two bowls.

"I keep wanting to say, what was he thinking, but

the only answer is that he wasn't. Thinking, I mean." Kass narrowed her gaze at Hailey's back. "Not only with the drunk driving, but being out with Dixie Wayling. How could he have conveniently forgotten she lives with Dan Ranta and had given birth to his baby only a few months before?"

It wasn't Kass's imagination. The muscles across Hailey's shoulders had tightened, visible through the white tank top.

"I wonder what he'll do when he gets out of jail. Jasmine and Peter bought out his share of Bridgeview Backyards so he could pay his fine. I wonder if they'll hire him on an hourly basis so he'll have a job at least." Kass couldn't stop now. Not when her usually curious, chatty cousin held her silence. "But he can't drive for two years, unless he gets one of those ignition interlock devices—"

"I know all that, okay?" Hailey's voice was taut. "It's not like we need to gossip."

Interesting. Hailey didn't usually mind a good gab fest. "I didn't think it was gossip. Daria is Basil's sister-in-law, and she was explaining to me how it all worked. It's not like his arrest is an unfounded, slanderous rumor. It happened, and it affects our community."

The microwave beeped. Kass opened it and removed the plate then buttered the four biscuits to the sound of silence from her cousin. With the food at the kitchen table, Hailey asked her to pray, after which she began eating.

Really? All this over Basil Santoro?

Kass took several bites of her chilled soup. "I find it interesting that you're so passionate about me not dating a single father when you obviously have your own hang-ups with men."

"No hang-ups."

"And here I thought flirting was your middle name."

"I don't flirt."

Kass's eyebrows lifted. "You've changed since Sunday?"

Her cousin glared. "With whom did I flirt on Sunday?"

"You were set to with Wesley until you realized he had a son."

"I wouldn't have. I only noticed there was someone new in church. That's all."

Laughter burst out. "Oh, come on, Hailey. Tell me why you don't want to talk about Basil. Got the hots for him?" That seemed so wrong. Basil was a player. Rude. Derisive.

"Of course not."

The reply was swift. Too swift. "Why, Hailey Ann. You do, too. When did that happen?"

Hailey shook her head. "You're reading way too much into this. Just because I don't want to gossip about him doesn't mean I'm languishing from unrequited love."

Unrequited love? Sounded serious.

"I feel kind of sorry for him, actually. His whole

family treats him like a pariah because he doesn't fit the Santoro mold. Granted, this isn't the best way to be seen as an individual, but can you blame him for rebelling, at least a little?"

Kass set down her spoon. The idea of empathizing with Basil seemed farfetched.

Hailey pressed her point. "You and I were both only children. We have no idea what kind of pressure a clan like the Santoros places on their members. Think of having Marietta for a grandmother. She does her best to rule every last one of them."

"Marietta?" Hailey was shifting gears quicker than Kass could keep up. "I adore Marietta. She's like a perfect, fragrant French loaf. Crusty on the outside, but soft and comforting on the inside."

"Can you imagine our grandparents trying to dictate every choice to us?"

"No..."

"Exactly. She twists her thumb and keeps them all in line."

"Except Basil. Oh, and Rob. He moved away years ago." Kass didn't know that particular cousin of Jasmine's well, but she'd heard all about him since he'd recently married and adopted his wife's children.

"Because Marietta kept interfering with his love life. Rob was perfectly capable of finding the right woman for him without his grandmother's assistance."

"One of Marietta's sons lives in Galena Landing,

too." Kass had gone to school with Tony Santoro, but they hadn't hung out in the same crowd.

"Very wise of him to keep his kids away from Marietta."

Kass rolled her eyes. "You make it sound like she's some evil witch. That's not how Jasmine sees her at all. She's a loving — if somewhat opinionated — grandmother who prays fervently for her family."

"Just saying it how I see it." Hailey spooned up a bite of gazpacho.

"And all this comes from trying to see life through Basil's eyes?"

"Good soup. We should add a couple of more chilled soups to the menu next summer."

CHAPTER 8

*W*esley pulled up in front of Bridgeview Bakery and Bistro as the glass door beneath the cheery yellow and white awning opened. Kass breezed through — she must have been watching for him — carrying a dark green backpack. She turned to say something to the woman behind her, who locked the door after Kass exited.

Wesley jogged around the truck and opened the passenger door for her. "Hey there. Can I set your pack in the backseat?" He caught the fragrance of something floral mingling with cinnamon, but restrained himself before leaning closer for a deeper whiff.

She slid the pack off her shoulder and handed it to him with a smile. "Thanks."

A moment later he climbed back into the driver's seat to find Kass turned to his son in the back. "Hey, Sebastian. What did you do today?"

"N-nothing much." Wesley imagined the slight shrug of his son's shoulder. "Played with T-Taz."

"I bet your kitty is a great playmate." She smiled.

And here Wesley had thought having his child along might put a damper on the date. But he was a package deal now, much different from the past few years when Sydney'd had custody, and Wesley only saw his son one weekend a month. It had been easy enough not to go out on those weekends — it wasn't like his social life had been that active, really.

Sydney's accusations rang in his ears. *All you do is work.*

Yeah, well. Not anymore, though the emails were piling up since he'd been distracted by the move and spending time with his son. Why did he think he had time to date when he had three orders due next week?

He glanced at Kass. She was why. He yearned for a partner, not just someone who could pick up the slack with the house and Sebastian... although that would be a nice side benefit.

Then her gaze caught his, and a little smile poked at her cheeks. Her red-gold hair cascaded past her shoulders and over the front of her peach-colored tank top in gentle curls instead of pulled back like usual. Were the strands as soft as they looked?

Wesley forced his attention back to the street as he circled uphill to the bridge access. Since when was he tongue-tied around women? He'd dated casually since the divorce, but everything had changed with Sydney's death. Forever looked a whole lot different than it had before, and drifting in and out of relationships wasn't going to cut it with Sebastian in his life full time.

Which raised the question, was Kass the kind of woman he could do permanence with? He glanced at her again. He couldn't afford to make a mistake, but he didn't know of any reason — yet — why Kass wasn't perfect.

The truck soared over the bridge across the Spokane River, Bridgeview beneath them, then past the newer subdivision of Kendall Yards.

It wasn't long before Sebastian spoke from the back. "Dad? Are we g-going to Gigi's place?"

Kass's eyebrows lifted as she turned toward him.

"No, buddy. Not today."

"Good."

Yeah, Wesley felt the same way. He needed Astrid and Robert, but not a steady dose.

"Who's Gigi?" Kass's voice was bland.

"Sebastian's grandmother."

"Oh." Kass seemed to settle deeper into her seat, her face turning pink.

Wait. What? He flashed her a grin. "Sydney's parents live on this side of the river. They help out some with Sebastian."

"I-I see."

Wesley reached across the center console and captured Kass's hand. "I meant it when I said there was no one special in my life. In our lives."

She stared down at his hand. Then she slowly slid hers out from beneath it and twisted her fingers together. "Sorry for jumping to conclusions."

He looked in the rearview mirror, where his son stared out the side window, seemingly not paying attention to the adults in the front or the fact that his father's hand rested on a pretty woman's knee. "I keep forgetting how awkward the first few dates are, while you get to know each other a bit." Yikes. Something else that had come out wrong. "Not that I've done a ton of dating since Sydney..."

"How long ago did she pass away?"

Reasonable question, but the answer wasn't as helpful as Kass might think. Another peek in the rearview mirror showed Sebastian's eyes meeting his.

Wesley withdrew his hand and let out a nervous chuckle. "It's a long story, and I'd rather tell it without little ears. Is there a playground at the park we're going to?"

She slowly shook her head. "No. I didn't think about that. There are hiking trails and a suspension bridge over the river, but no place for a child to play independently."

He did a quick map survey in his head. "How about we stop at Cannon Park for a bit first? It's right on the way, and I can tell you my life story while he plays."

"Okay. That sounds good." Kass glanced at him. "Not that you have to tell me everything."

"Kass, I like you, but there are things you need to know before we get in any deeper. I hate putting disclaimers up front, but—" he thumbed toward the backseat "—getting some things in the open is probably a good idea before he gets any ideas." Who was he kidding? Disclaimers up front was probably a bad idea. She'd tell him a polite *thanks, but no thanks.* He'd only see her at the cooking club after this, and church if he decided to keep going. At the bistro and around the neighborhood. Okay, it could be awkward, but it wasn't like he'd kissed her. Yet. He'd been thinking about her pretty lips, and how soft and tasty they'd be under his. Which was all kinds of ridiculous, because she was sure to run.

Yeah. They needed to have this uncomfortable talk sooner rather than later.

As soon as Wesley let his son out of the backseat, the boy dashed toward the playground structure. Kass frowned as she followed beside Wesley. It seemed out of character for the shy child.

Wesley nudged her shoulder with his. "Guess this is where I tell you that he's been here before. His grandparents live just a couple of blocks away."

"I see." She took a deep breath and let it out slowly. Why did she find herself attracted to men with children? They complicated everything. Not just their own presence, but the ghost of their mother and the additional extended family.

Hailey was right. She should look for a guy without baggage. As far as she knew, she was perfectly capable of conceiving and giving birth, not that the opportunity had presented itself. It wasn't like a ready-made family was her only chance to have children.

Sebastian climbed a series of rungs bolted onto poles and emerged, victorious, on the structure's deck before running across and scooting into an enclosed slide.

Sure, Kass's unborn children needed their mother, but so did this precious little guy. Wesley was right. She needed to know what she was getting into.

He took her hand and guided her to a nearby picnic table in the shade, where he climbed onto the table with his feet on the bench.

She joined him, leaving a few inches between them, and clasped her hands in her lap. "Okay. I'm listening."

"I met Sydney at a nightclub in Portland. That's the kind of life we both led back then."

No judging. History is history.

"We connected deeper than the party level, though, and I proposed when we found out she was pregnant. I figured we could overcome our rocky start and build a solid life together."

Kass could feel Wesley's gaze brush her face, but she feigned complete absorption in watching Sebastian, who was on his way down the slide for the third time.

"It went okay for a couple of years, though she dabbled in drugs. I'd quit because I needed a stable job to take care of my family. Providing everything I could for Sydney and Sebastian became my new addiction. I worked hard, with long hours of overtime at the plant."

What was with men? Kass's dad had been the same, thinking it was more important to provide toys than time.

"Sydney wanted it all, plus my undivided attention. Of course, that was impossible. I know I didn't do everything right, but I did try."

Wesley sounded so miserable, Kass couldn't help turning to him. He stared off into the distance with unseeing eyes. She touched his hand. "I'm sure you did."

He blinked and refocused on her, curling his fingers around hers. "Sydney took Sebastian and left before his second birthday. I had to work even longer hours to pay child support as well as keep a roof over my own head. I began creating art as a side income." He squeezed her hand. "Apparently people liked the result. In less than a year, I'd quit my job and never looked back."

"I have no trouble believing that," she said quietly. Should she remove her hand? It might send the wrong message... like leaving it in place didn't?

"Sydney stopped laughing at my dreams about then. She hinted that she'd have my child support level assessed but, before she could talk to her lawyer, she died."

Kass's heart clenched. "Oh, no."

"Please know I never wanted to withhold anything Sebastian needed." Anguish filled his voice. "He meant everything to me then, and he does now. I just didn't want to fund Sydney's lifestyle."

"Of course, you didn't." Her thumb rubbed circles on his hand like it had a mind of its own.

"She left Sebastian with friends in Newport and headed toward Bandon, where I was living at the time. She was high on weed, but wanted to see for herself what she could claim. She drifted into oncoming traffic on 101 and was mowed over by a northbound RV." Wesley pulled his hands away and cradled his face with them. His shoulders trembled.

Was it from the trauma, or had he still loved his ex-wife? Kass didn't know, but she did know he needed comfort. She scooted a little closer and rested her arm across his shoulders.

"Witnesses say the RV driver laid on his horn to get her attention, but her path didn't veer at all. He saw her eyes focus in the split second before the crash." Wesley's voice broke as he leaned against Kass. "She died instantly. There wasn't much left of her Accord."

"The driver of the RV?"

Wesley rubbed his face. "In the hospital for a few weeks, but came through okay."

She nodded and bit her lip. "I'm sorry about Sydney."

He gave a harsh laugh and glanced toward the playground. "I'd spent nearly four years living for the weekend every month when I had Sebastian. I'd been gathering information to get the judge's ruling over-turned, to prove I was the better parent for our son to live with. And then, in the blink of an eye, she was gone."

"And your dream came true, but at a high price."

He shook his head. "It wasn't that easy. Sydney had fed her parents all sorts of lies about me, and they chal-lenged my rights in court."

"No way."

"That's why I live in Spokane now. So they can watch and be satisfied that I'm taking good care of Sebastian."

"That's crazy, to have every move scrutinized." Was someone spying on them even now? He'd said they lived nearby. Maybe they watched from one of the many windows facing the park and were, even now, looking her up online. Kass pulled her arm away.

"They're good people. Well, they have their idiosyn-crasies, but they mean well." Wesley leaned back, his hands braced on the picnic table, his arm pressing against Kass's back.

"How about *your* parents? Are they in the picture?"

"No."

Wow, that had been a short, sharp answer, but he seemed disinclined to elaborate. "I can't imagine never seeing my parents."

Wesley angled a look at her. "Do they live in Bridgeview?"

"No. I grew up in Galena Landing, a small town in northern Idaho. I visit often, or they come here."

"Siblings?"

"None. I think that's why my cousin, Hailey, and I have always been close. There was no one else for either of us."

Silence stretched for a long moment. Kass watched Sebastian climb a metal corkscrew and spin back down in circles.

Wesley reached around her with a quick hug then let go. "He's going to be over here any minute asking for food. Are you still up for spending more time with us?"

He was really asking if his history and current circumstances had tossed up red flags she couldn't get past. He wondered if his son's heart was safe with her. If his own was, because they'd been rejected enough.

She'd been hurt, too. As a child, but her mind veered away from those memories. She'd been hurt by Mason's rejection, by how quickly his twins latched onto Liz when Kass was no longer in the picture. Little Avery had been a sponge for affection.

Sebastian ran toward the picnic table but tripped over something in the sand. Wesley surged toward his son faster than Kass could blink, scooping him up and whirling him around. The boy giggled with his arms around his daddy's neck then climbed around for a piggy-back ride.

Wesley reached his hand toward Kass.

Time stood still.

Would she step forward and see what the future held, or would she protect herself? She was twenty-eight years old. She'd achieved the major goal of owning her own successful business — with Hailey, of course. Shouldn't she give her other dream a chance? Of being a wife? A mom?

Kass slid off the picnic table and dusted off the seat of her shorts. She strode toward the father and son and took Wesley's hand in hers. His grip was warm. Strong. She looked over at Sebastian as she bumped shoulders with his dad. "Did you have fun?"

The boy nodded enthusiastically. "Yeah, b-but I'm hungry."

"Me, too, little bean. Me, too."

CHAPTER 9

*W*esley stood beside the river beyond his backyard, one arm wrapped around Kass's waist. "Thanks for taking us to the Bowl and Pitcher today. The suspension bridge was a big hit with Sebastian."

Kass giggled. "How many times did he run across it, anyway?"

He had no idea. A lot. "We're a pair of nature boys. I've taken him camping and fishing every chance I've had." He made a face. "Ironically, that's been fewer times this summer since I've had him full time. Everything's been in upheaval."

She cast him a side-eye. "You like the outdoors?"

"Love it. Living along the river makes the city bearable." He leaned closer to her ear. "Don't tell Sebastian, but sometimes when he's asleep at night I cast a line in the river back here. I've caught a couple of redbands, too small to keep. Promise I'm never out of sight of the house and Sebastian's window."

"I love fishing."

Had he heard her correctly? Sydney's only interest in fish had been pan-seared halibut at an upscale restaurant. "Oh, yeah?"

"I used to fish with my dad a lot."

Wesley could barely hear her quiet voice over the churn of the river. "Used to?"

Kass shrugged slightly as she stared downstream. "We're not exactly neighbors, with him in Idaho and me in the city."

"You can come down here and toss a line in any time you like. Do you use a fly or a spinning reel?"

"Fly, mostly." She glanced at him. "Jasmine and I fish around the bend sometimes. Only, this summer, she's been kind of distracted with planning a wedding and all."

He slid his hand up and down her side. "I meant it. Come over any time." He nuzzled her hair, filled with the fragrance of strawberries. "My buddy and I would love to join you. We get enough, we can have a fish fry."

Kass turned slightly and met his gaze. "I'd really like that."

Was it his imagination, or did those words mean more? Only one way to find out if she felt the same way he did, or was simply humoring him. "Me, too. I really like *you*, Kassidy North."

"But we barely know each other."

"That's what dating is for." His fingers brushed her cheek. "You know more about me than you did yesterday and, yet, for some strange reason, we're here. You didn't beg me to take you home after hearing my sordid tale at Cannon Park."

"True." Her eyes searched his.

"You haven't told me your story yet. Why a gorgeous, successful woman like you is still single. Or single again."

She drew back slightly. "I don't switch relationships like changing clothes or even hairstyles."

Like he'd thought. Wesley tangled his fingers in the curls tumbling over her shoulders. Did he make a wise-crack about different hairstyles? Probably not, when she looked so serious.

"I don't do casual. For me, love is a forever thing. That's what I'm looking for."

And he'd been in more relationships than he could count, though not all of them deserved that title. He'd thought Sydney would be forever, but she'd left him in two ways, divorce and then death. What did forever mean, anyway?

The intensity in those brown eyes sucked him in. "I can try forever," he whispered. "It's the perfect goal."

"Do or not do. There is no try."

"Yoda." Wesley couldn't help the chuckle that escaped. "Never figured you for a Star Wars fan."

"And why not? There's a lot you don't know about me."

He cupped her face in both hands. "I want to learn." He leaned closer and tasted her lips.

She pulled back slightly, but her hands rested on his hips. "I've never been married. Never been in love. Not really."

Whoa. He'd better tread mighty carefully here. That meant she had physical lines he'd better not cross, but he'd already figured that since she went to church. Why was she even remotely interested in him after his disclosure? She'd probably never done a thing wrong.

Maybe the bigger question was why he was interested in her. She wasn't the kind of girl he usually went for. Sydney would have howled with laughter at the thought of attending church. Yeah, he'd gone the first time because of his neighbors' invitation, but he'd returned every Sunday since then because they all seemed to be genuinely nice people and because Pastor Tomas made him think.

Maybe there was more to life than how he'd been living, going from party boy to workaholic. This new season, full-time caretaker for a six-year-old, required some adjustments, and church had seemed like a reasonable addition, especially when he considered that a good percentage of his neighbors could be found there every Sunday morning.

Would that be enough for Kassidy? It was all he knew, so it would have to be. "What is love, really?" he asked.

Kass studied him thoughtfully. "Love is patient. Love is kind. Love is—"

"That's in the Bible, isn't it?" How much should he admit? "I, uh, don't really know my Bible that well."

She nodded. "First Corinthians thirteen, known as the love chapter. It lists so many beautiful characteristics of love. One of them is that love never fails. That's what I mean by forever love."

Wesley's thumbs grazed her cheekbones. "I'll look it up and give it a read through." Learning what she thought love was all about was probably a good idea, because he could catch a glimpse of a future with her. It didn't hurt that she was the polar opposite of Sydney. Beautiful instead of cute. Serious instead of playful. Mature instead of bratty.

He didn't even need to lean, since she was near his height. He touched his lips to hers and, when she didn't pull away, gathered her in his arms. She fit perfectly. She tasted so good, a combination of fried chicken, the mint gum she'd popped in after their picnic, and a flavor all her own. He groaned and deepened the kiss as her arms slid around his waist.

He'd do anything to keep her in his life permanently. She was the stability his life needed. She was the other half of his soul.

KASS PROBABLY SHOULDN'T BE KISSING him like this,

but she didn't want to stop. Wesley was the real deal, and he liked her. It would take a master manipulator to look at her the way he did, to speak the words he did, and to kiss with this much passion if she'd only built things up in her imagination.

She'd kissed Mason Waterman back in Galena Landing, but it hadn't been mutual, not like this. He'd been trying to let her down gently. She'd kissed a boyfriend or two before Mason, but she'd known those relationships weren't going anywhere. At least, she wasn't going where the guys wanted to take her. It had all been physical. A conquest.

As she responded to Wesley's kiss, giving as well as taking, she could feel the difference. Yes, there was a tiny warning bell ringing in the back of her brain, but she silenced it. He might be more experienced than she was, but it wasn't like he was going to ravish her here and now.

Yes, it was too early to speak of love, of permanence, but it didn't stop her soul from peering through the window to the possibility. How would she know if she didn't take the chance?

But when Wesley's lips trailed down her throat, she pushed away just enough to send the message he'd gone far enough. He branded one eyelid and then the other before nuzzling her neck through her hair with a groan. "What're you doing to me, woman?"

This wasn't how it was supposed to be. She edged

back a little farther, and his hands dropped to her waist as he peered into her eyes in the moonlight.

"I'm sorry, Kass. I didn't mean to push my luck." He swept his lips over hers once again.

What on earth did he mean? Kass pushed out of the circle of his arms, leaned against the fence separating his backyard from the riverbank, and tried to find her voice. "I didn't mean to send the wrong message." Although... had she?

He turned and rested his elbows on the fence beside her, his muscled arm pressed against hers. "What message do you mean?"

Lord, help me here. I'm in over my head. "When I said I was looking for my forever love, I meant I was waiting for him. That I believe God will honor my commitment to wait for marriage."

Silence stretched so long she snuck a peek at him. He stared out onto the river as an owl hooted in the distance. Finally he turned to her, eyebrows raised. "Then God is a spoilsport."

"Pardon me?" Kass stepped aside, the August night suddenly chill. She wrapped both arms around herself.

Wesley shook his head. "Sorry. I forgot what different worlds we come from. I'm trying here, Kass."

"I'm not sure what you mean."

"This God thing. I'm not used to thinking about Him. Considering His opinion on things. Reading the Bible."

"But... you go to church." *Stupid, Kass. You know*

going to church doesn't make a person a Christian any more than sitting in the bistro makes one a cinnamon roll.

"Myles invited me. It's been interesting." He searched her face. "Sydney's mother thinks I've lost my marbles."

Wow. When he said it was all new to him, he meant really new. And somehow, she'd lost touch with Christian Dating 101, making sure the other party was a believer before she went out with him. Before she kissed him. What a kiss, though. She wanted more of that, but not as much as she wanted to do the right thing.

"I'm sorry. I think it's vital for a couple to be going in the same direction before they commit to each other."

"Same direction?" He looked genuinely confused.

"Forever's a long time, Wesley. It goes beyond our life here on earth to eternity."

∽⌒⌒

WESLEY STARED AT KASS. What kind of mystic voodoo was she talking about? "You mean... reincarnation?" Because that was just ridiculous.

"What? No. That's not what I said at all. I meant that our existence doesn't end when we die. It's not that we get recycled into another being. It's that our life here sets the stage for eternity. What we believe, how we live, matters. If we believe in Jesus, if we accept

His sacrifice and follow His direction in our lives, we'll spend eternity in heaven with Him."

This was getting weirder and weirder. Maybe pursuing Kassidy North was a mistake on his part. He was busy enough integrating his business with being a full-time father. He didn't have time to waste on a dead-end relationship contemplating the mysteries of the universe. All forever meant was wrapped up in the wedding vow, *as long as we both shall live.* How could Kass think it went beyond that?

She took another step back. "I should probably be going."

He hadn't been thinking. He'd picked her up for their picnic and then brought her back to his place, where he'd tucked Sebastian in bed. Her apartment was several long blocks away, and there was no neighborhood safe enough for a woman to walk home alone in the dark. Had he thought she'd spend the night? No, he'd known better than that, at least on a first date. Especially with Kass. She was different. "Let me call you a cab."

"It's okay. I'll walk."

"But..."

She shrugged, not meeting his gaze. "I've walked Bridgeview a thousand times. It's fine."

"I insist." He thumbed on his phone, looked up the number, and made the call. Then he reached for her.

She tucked her hands in her shorts' pockets and

started up the path toward his house and the street beyond.

He fell into step beside her. "Look, I'm sorry. I didn't think this religion thing would be a deal breaker. I'm willing to keep going to church every week. It's kind of interesting." So long as Pastor Tomas steered clear of the weird stuff.

Kass didn't say anything more until she stood on the curb. "I'm really sorry, Wesley. I had no business going out with you without knowing we were on the same page."

"I don't get it. I said I'll give it a try."

She shook her head. "I want you to, but I'm not a good enough reason."

"How can you say that?" She was beautiful. Kind. Patient. All the things she'd said about the love chapter. She was reason enough for anything, even the odd bits.

"Wesley, this thing is between you and God, first of all. Talk to Pastor Tomas." She poked her chin toward the house next door, where all the lights were already off. "Talk to Myles, or Marco, maybe. But find out what the Bible is all about. Who Jesus is, and how much He loves you. That's got to come first. Not because of me, but because your heart resonates with that message."

Several blocks away, a yellow car with a sign on top turned onto his street. He only had a minute to make sense of Kass's words. He grasped her hands, but she didn't come closer. "Kass, I'll do it. Anything. I promise."

The cab veered to a stop beside them.

Kass smiled at him, but her lips trembled. "Take care, Wesley. I'll see you around."

Only when the cab pulled away did he realize he hadn't paid for it... and had no idea what had just happened.

CHAPTER 10

*K*ass paid the cabbie and, with shaking fingers, punched in the code for the door lock at the back of the building. How could she have been so stupid? She knew better. She *knew* better. How could the perfect guy for her not even be a believer? She'd let him kiss her. More than that, she'd kissed him back, dreaming of forever with stars in her eyes.

It was too much to hope that Hailey had already gone to bed at barely past ten, but what could Kass tell her? She tried to compose herself as she climbed the stairs to the apartment and nudged the door open quietly, only to hear voices. Oh, no. Even worse, Hailey had someone over. Was there any hope of sidling through the corner of the living room and down the hallway without being spotted?

"There she is now."

Still out of sight, Kass froze. *Lord, please. Couldn't You give me a little time to compose myself?*

"Hey, Kass? Guess who's here."

Apparently God's answer was negative. Kass dashed the tears from her eyes and forced a smile to her lips as she stepped into the doorway. "I'm back."

Her stepmother rose from Kass's favorite chair. "Honey, I tried to call."

Kass crossed the room and hugged her. "I'm sorry. I had my phone turned off. Have you been here long?"

Mom smiled as she hugged her back. "A couple of hours. Hailey's been entertaining me."

"I told her all about your hot date." Hailey smirked.

"Um, thanks." Awkward. But what was Lenore doing here, anyway? She never came to Spokane without Dad, and even that was rare. But to arrive in the evening without calling in advance? Trying to phone when she was already on the way didn't count. Not from a woman who didn't do spontaneous.

Kass raised her brows at her stepmom. "Is everything okay?"

Hailey stood to her feet. "Nice to see you, Aunt Lenore. I'll be in my room if you need anything." She nudged Kass on her way by. "You can tell me all about Wonderful Wesley in the morning." Then she disappeared into the bathroom.

"Mom? You're making me nervous."

"Maybe we should sit down."

As though that would comfort her, but Kass

obliged. Anything to get her stepmom talking. Anything to keep a second lump from joining the first one in her gut.

Mom perched on the edge of Hailey's chair and clasped her hands together before looking over at Kass. "I left your father."

Kass blinked. "You *what?*"

"I-I know that might seem rather extreme, but I couldn't take being invisible anymore."

Oh, Lord. What do we do now? Did she even want to know the details of her father's second marriage? But she wasn't a child anymore; she was an adult, and her stepmother had come to her. Dad hadn't. Lenore had.

She took a deep breath. "What happened?"

Lenore poked at a thread in the hem of her shorts. "He never notices if I'm there or not, unless it's meal-time. He's so busy with work and the Lions club and the rod and gun club and... everything." She waved a hand. "We've just grown apart, and he doesn't love me anymore."

Kass's brain reeled. "Did he say that?" Because she'd give him a kick in the shins if he had. Lenore had been the best thing that ever happened to him after Mom's death. Best thing that had ever happened to Kass.

"No." Lenore shook her head. "He'd have to be home to say anything at all."

"I don't get it. What are you going to do?"

"I don't know. I didn't think beyond coming to you. He hasn't phoned?"

Kass dug out her cell and turned it on. There'd been several missed calls from Lenore's number, but none from Dad's. She shook her head. "Sorry, no."

"I didn't think so." Lenore sighed. "I know it's an imposition, but can I stay with you and Hailey for a few days while I try to figure things out? Put me to work. I'm happy to help out."

"We do have a spare room, as you know." Kass eyed her stepmother. "And we do have a desperate need for more staff in the bistro. One of our full-timers broke her leg a couple of weeks ago and is out until the middle of September, most likely."

Lenore straightened in the chair. "I can step in. I can wipe tables and run the till. Not so sure about baking."

"Hailey's got the kitchen covered. It's front-end staff we need."

"Let me help. Please."

"We'll pay you, of course."

"No need."

"I insist, and so will Hailey. No one works for us for free. Your shift is Tuesday through Saturday, ten to six, and includes scrubbing counters and washing floors after closing."

Lenore blinked. "You really do need someone."

"We really do."

"For a month."

Kass nodded.

Lenore rose to her feet and extended her hand. "Then I'm your girl."

"Good. That's a load off my mind, and I know it will be a relief to Hailey, too. We've had a lot of students apply, but we need someone more mature who can work daytime hours once school goes back in next week." Of course, as soon as Dad came to his senses, Mom would head back to Galena Landing, but in the meanwhile, her presence downstairs would be a huge help.

"Your cousin tells me you've met a great guy. Wesley, she said?"

Kass stared into her stepmom's eyes like a coon caught in a headlight. "I don't think it will work out."

"Oh, no. I'm sorry to hear that."

"He... I... I'm not sure what to say. We had a good time tonight. He's got a little boy, Sebastian."

"You always did have a soft spot for kids."

Maybe it was the bad-boy vibe she was attracted to. After all, neither Wesley nor Mason before him had been happily married and widowed. Mason had acquired his twins through riotous living, as the Bible might say, and Wesley had been divorced before his wife died. What did that say about Kass? That she saw men with kids like a rescue project only she could fix?

Kass shook the thought right out of her head. That was ludicrous. She was looking for love with someone who loved Jesus first and her second. Wesley wasn't that person, and she couldn't allow his sweet little boy's puppy-dog eyes to sway her. "Anyway, we met here at the bistro and then again at church. I assumed... I assumed he was a believer because I've seen him in church a few times. Tonight was our first and last date. I discovered he doesn't, in fact, know Jesus." And for just a few minutes, she almost hadn't cared, she was that hungry for love.

"I'm sorry, honey. Does it help to hear that it's better to know that now than later?"

Yeah, Dad had faked an interest for Lenore's sake back when Kass was a kid. He'd gone to church most of the time for a few years and learned the lingo, but it'd been mostly to keep his wife happy. Kass had been a teen before she figured it out, though. He'd been pretty convincing. "It sort of helps. But tonight... tonight everything simply hurts."

Lenore gave her a hug. "I'll pray for you, and I hope you'll pray for your dad and me, too. I don't know what to do."

"Thanks, and you've got it." Kass's gaze collided with the clock on the wall. "I need to get to bed. Did you bring your bags upstairs?"

Lenore nodded, pointing to two pieces of luggage beside the door.

"You know where the guest room is. I've got opening shift tomorrow, so I'll be downstairs by six. Help yourself to anything in the fridge or cupboard for breakfast, or come on down if you like. Either way, I'll watch for you by ten to help you get started. If you're serious."

"Thank you. I'm definitely serious."

Now if Kass could only get to sleep. She had a funny feeling she'd be reliving Wesley's kiss for half the night.

WESLEY WHIPPED his fly rod then let the weighted line settle onto the black river. Where had the evening gone wrong? Definitely not where he'd thought it might, with his confessions of life with Sydney.

He felt the current tug the fly downstream. Wasn't that just life? No matter what he did, how hard he tried, everything swept away. If God was real, there ought to be more purpose. Kass seemed to think there was, but maybe she saw what she wanted to see. She had some interesting ideas on forever, but Wesley knew better.

His life with Sydney hadn't ended with their divorce. He'd still had to meet her to hand their son back and forth. Her personality and games still affected him, even if not on a daily or even hourly basis like when they'd been together.

Death was more final. He didn't have to deal with her anymore, but the aftermath remained. Her death had left him with a vulnerable child and a pair of interfering ex-in-laws who figured they knew what was best for his son, even while they barely lifted a finger to help.

In that way, Kass was right. Sydney's reach was beyond her grave. Her effect on her parents, on Wesley, and on their son remained as long as they lived, and probably for generations to come.

He reeled in the line and cast it again.

That's not what Kass meant, though. She seemed to think there was actual life after death, not just lingering effects.

With blackness all around him, he might as well be standing by a remote stream. Across the river lay a conservation area unlit by manmade lights. The murmurs of night surrounded him — the hoots and replies of owls, an occasional bullfrog's croak, the yip of a distant coyote. A bat swooped, barely visible, black on black.

How could a guy know if there really was a God? That seemed the first question requiring an answer, before he could worry about life after death or even whether God cared about sex between consenting adults.

"God? You out there?"

Wesley's voice seemed swallowed up in the surrounding stillness, like he'd spoken into an unending void.

Did he expect an answer? Wouldn't he be shocked if a booming voice replied! Or even a whisper. Still, it seemed his question sat poised on the edge of an invisible precipice.

He cleared his throat and spoke again, louder this time. "If You're real, God, I could use some answers. I'd really like to know."

Yeah, he was crazy, talking to himself on the banks of the river late at night. Because it was obvious the Big Guy wasn't listening. How could He be, when He wasn't real?

"Good question, Wesley."

He lurched a step upriver toward the voice. That had been real. Audible. It sounded a whole lot like his neighbor, actually. Oh, man. Wesley's face burned. Of all the stupid things for Myles Sheridan to overhear, Wesley talking to an absentee God had to be about the dumbest.

"If that was an honest question, neighbor, God will answer you." Twigs cracked and dry grass rustled as Myles moved toward him along the riverfront.

"Yeah, sorry. A moment of weakness." Wesley cringed even as the words came out of his mouth. Myles was a churchgoer. Nothing like burning bridges tonight with every conversation he participated in.

A shadow that could only be Myles came to a stop beside him. "I don't think a man asks that question in a moment of weakness. He asks it in a moment of searching. Of questioning the meaning of life."

Wesley let out an awkward chuckle. "Maybe."

"Do you have a Bible?"

"Uh..." Did he? Probably not.

"Don't worry about it. You can download it as a free app. Try the English Standard Version or maybe the Passion translation. Look for the book of John and read it. But before you start, ask that question again. Ask God if He's real, and if He'd show Himself to you."

"You're serious."

"Sure am. It's one of the most important questions you'll ever ask, so be sure you're listening for the answer. One thing's certain. If the question is sincere, the answer will come."

"That sounds a little weird, to be honest."

Myles chuckled. "I can see how it would seem that way. But give it a try. What have you got to lose?" He took a few steps back toward his house.

What did he have to lose, indeed? Not much. But maybe he had a lot to gain. Like Kass, though she said a relationship was a bad reason for faith. Okay, well, he still had a lot to gain, potentially.

Myles paused. "One more thing?"

"Yeah?"

"If you've got any questions while you're reading along, feel free to ask me. I can't promise I know the answers, but I'll give it my best shot."

"Thanks. I appreciate it."

The sounds of his neighbor backtracking through the cottonwoods to the house next door diminished as Wesley reeled in his line one last time, eyeing the black sky. "Okay, God. You're on."

He turned toward the house just in time to see a meteor streaking through the eastern sky. Sure, it was part of the Perseids shower. He'd seen tons of falling stars over the years in mid-August. But this one was brighter than most, and this one seemed to carry a message.

Was God telling Wesley He was the real deal?

*H*ey, you okay?" Dusted in flour to her elbows, Hailey paused at the baking table. "Sorry to hit you with that last night after your hot date."

Kass took a deep breath. "It wasn't so hot."

Hailey rolled out the dough as the fragrances of coffee and cinnamon already mingled and flooded the space. "I thought you really liked this guy. I can't even remember last time you went out."

"He's not a Christian." Kass poured herself a coffee from the staff pot. Today warranted black. It would take all the caffeine in creation to keep her alert after tossing and turning all night. Her mind had ricocheted from Wesley's amazing kiss to the discovery he didn't know God to the shocking revelation that her parents' marriage was in trouble. Her stepmom was a believer. If it hadn't been for Lenore's influence, where would Kass be now?

"You're kidding me. But he goes to church..."

"Yeah, I know. I should've asked more questions before assuming anything."

Hailey reached for the bowl of soft butter and began smearing it liberally across the dough. "At least you found out before you fell in love." She glanced up, eyebrows raised. "Right?"

The back door opened again, and Celeste strolled in, snapping her gum. She looked from Kass to Hailey to the clock. "I'm not late, am I?"

Whew. Kass didn't need to admit anything to Hailey, at least not now. "Right on time. It's seven. I'm sure the regulars are waiting." She set the cash tray in the register and turned it on, while Celeste flipped on the bank of light switches and made her way through the quiet eating area to the front door.

As soon as Celeste unlocked it, several people entered. Linnea's brother Dan strode straight to the sales counter and handed his travel mug to Kass.

"Good morning, Dan. The usual?"

"Please."

She prepped his Americano while Celeste assembled two hot egg sandwiches and a still warm cinnamon roll. "Have a busy day planned?"

"Ten hours at least of mowing lawns and clipping hedges."

Kass glanced over at him as she set his items on the

counter. "Business is good, then?" He'd taken over the family landscaping firm last fall after his dad's heart attack and had been veering it toward more environmentally friendly practices.

"Can't complain."

He looked like he wanted to, though, by the taciturn expression on his face. Kass paused. Now that Linnea and Logan — Dan's sister and brother-in-law — had moved to Edmonds for college, was there anyone in his life showing Jesus to this man and his family? Not something Kass could step into. Not with Dan having a live-in girlfriend. Maybe she should try harder to befriend Dixie, but the woman was annoying. Was that simply because she didn't know the Lord? Kass filed the thought for later as she swiped Dan's debit card through the machine. "Take care. See you tomorrow."

He nodded and turned away before stopping and facing her. "Know of any rental houses in Bridgeview? Our apartment is too far from most of the business's clients, plus I hate storing all the lawn equipment at my parents' place."

Kass could imagine. Dave Ranta Senior was a very unpleasant man, to put it lightly. "Hmm. Marietta's house that Logan and Jacob rented?" Both guys were now married, and the house sat empty, last Kass had heard.

Dan snorted as he shook his head. "She won't rent it to me. I already asked, but since Dixie isn't my wife, the old lady more or less slammed the door in my face."

"Oh. That's too bad." It kind of made sense, at least coming from Marietta, but that didn't help Dan any, either in the housing situation or helping draw him closer to the Lord. "If I hear of anything else, I'll let you know."

"Thanks." He headed for the door.

Kass turned to the next customer, a woman who picked up a hazelnut latte and cinnamon roll every day on her way to work. When she and Celeste had filled that order, Jasmine's brother Alex was next in his black slacks and tie with a light gray button-down.

"Hey, Kass."

"Hi, Alex. How's the number crunching?" Alex was a CPA at a large accounting firm downtown.

He grinned at her. "Saving the world one number at a time."

"Nice." She laughed. "Are there any houses for rent in your part of town? Dan Ranta is looking for someplace with enough room to park his mowers and such."

Alex pursed his lips. "I can't think of any, but some might be coming on the market or for rent as their elderly owners age out of living alone. Peter's planning to buy Mrs. Essery's house as soon as she decides to sell, but there are other seniors getting toward that stage. I'm guessing Dan would be hoping for an option to buy down the road?"

"Good guess, but I didn't ask."

"I'll keep an ear open."

"Thanks." Kass rang up his order.

The routine settled into place. A few customers ate in, so Celeste bussed tables. Shay came in at nine and worked beside Hailey in the kitchen, prepping Friday's standing orders for pickup.

Kass looked up to find Lenore as her next customer. "Good morning. I hope you slept well."

Her stepmom shrugged slightly, her eyes tired. "Not too bad, all things considered. It's a lovely guest room, thank you."

"Have you had breakfast, or can I get you something?"

Lenore looked up at the menu board. "I'm not very hungry, but I suppose I should eat something. How about a Denver on sourdough, and a plain coffee?"

"Sure. I'll come sit with you. I'm due for a break anyway. Celeste can take over for a bit." She beckoned the younger woman closer. "I'd like you to meet my stepmom, Lenore. She's going to be working here, so I need you to show her around when she starts her shift at ten, okay?"

"Um, sure. I can do that."

Kass set two Denver sandwiches and two coffees on the table Lenore had chosen along the back wall. Right under the display of Wesley's work.

"You have such a lovely little café." Lenore took it all in then focused on the metal sculptures on the whitewashed planks. "Interesting artwork. Is that a saw blade?"

"Yes. This... artist creates all kinds of pieces from

old car parts and tools and found objects. His work is quite popular throughout the Pacific Northwest. He moved to Spokane recently, and we're lucky to show-case his designs for the next couple of months." There. She'd kept her voice casual, hadn't she?

Lenore took a sip of coffee then reached for a rack card. "Wesley Ferguson," she read aloud then raised her eyebrows at Kass. "This wouldn't be the same Wesley you went out with?"

The bells over the door jangled as someone entered the bistro. Someone who was Wesley. Kass's heart paused then sped up. No amount of telling herself she couldn't allow herself to be interested in him made any difference. That ship had sailed before the toe-curling kiss last night in his backyard.

But she couldn't succumb, either. She only needed to look across the table at Lenore to remember how marriage to a man weak in faith could play out. She'd have looked at her stepmother if she could, but her eyes refused to obey. They stayed riveted to Wesley until his gaze snapped to hers.

⁓

KASS LOOKED AMAZING, but then, she always did. Wait, were her eyes puffy? Had she had as much trouble sleeping last night as he had? Her words had bounced through his head for hours. *Forever's a long time, Wesley.* He knew that. Forever was a very big word, but he didn't want to think what the rest of his life would look like without Kass in it. He'd only known her for a couple of weeks. Only kissed her once, but his soul had connected to hers on the deepest level.

Except the one she thought mattered most.

Wesley took two steps toward her before he realized she wasn't alone at the table. She sat across from a fiftyish woman who openly regarded him before glancing at Kass then back, eyebrows raised. Whoever she was, she knew something. He probably shouldn't go over there, but wouldn't that look strange, since he was halfway across the bistro already?

No, he was committed. For better or for worse. Great. He was even thinking in wedding vows. "Good morning, Kass. Mind if I join you for a minute?"

Wait. What?

She sucked in her lips and looked down at her hands, which turned her coffee cup in slow circles. "Sure."

He grabbed a vibrant yellow chair from a vacant table nearby, spun it, and straddled it. "I brought in a few pieces to replace the ones that've sold."

"Good plan." Kass gave a fleeting grin that might have been a grimace. "Wesley, I'd like you to meet my stepmother, Lenore. Lenore, this is Wesley." She thumbed at the cardinal on the wall beside them. "The artist."

The artist. Not the boyfriend. He hadn't even

earned the second title before it had been stripped from him.

"I'm pleased to meet you, Wesley. I was just commenting on your unique style to Kass." The older woman gave a small chuckle. "I should invite you to our farm in Idaho. I'm sure you could build a lot of sculptures from the old equipment abandoned behind our barn."

Kass gave her stepmother a sharp look.

Whatever that was about. Invitations like this had been goldmines for him in the past. Farmers often had amazing scrap metal stashed in the weeds. "Sounds great. We'll have to plan on it sometime."

Lenore's chair scraped as she rose. "It's almost ten o'clock. You said Celeste would be training me?"

Kass nodded. "Tell her I'll watch the counter while she shows you around."

Wesley angled his head as the woman walked away. "She works here? I thought they lived in Idaho." In fact, she'd just said so. Hadn't she? He scratched his neck.

Kass closed her eyes. "She was here when I got home last night. It seems she left my dad."

Oh. "I'm sorry to hear that."

"Me, too. I know they've had some issues, but..."

"Have they... were they married long?"

"Over twenty years." She took a sip of her coffee, the mug trembling in her hand. "I barely remember my mom. She died of cancer when I was four. Lenore rescued me. Rescued my dad." Tears glistened on her lashes.

Why couldn't Wesley gather her into his arms and kiss those tears away? Public place. Check. Also, she'd told him no last night. Said they had no future. He didn't want to check that box. Didn't that mean agreement? "You two must be really close, if she came to you."

She nodded, eyes still closed. "Should I let him know where she is? He hasn't called looking for her."

"He probably doesn't want to worry you, hoping it will blow over, and you'll never need to know."

"He hasn't called her, either."

"Oh." That put a different spin on it. "Kass, about last night."

She surged to her feet. "I should get back to work. There's a lot that needs to be done."

Wesley laid his hand over hers on the back of her chair. "I just want you to know I'm thinking about it, okay? Read that bit you mentioned to me." And a bunch more. He drove his other hand through his hair. "That's a lot to live up to. All that *love is* stuff."

Her brown eyes caught on his. "That's great." But her voice was nearly flat. Devoid of emotion.

He angled his head. "Is that all? I thought you'd be happier than that." He'd counted on it, actually. Yeah, he'd read some in John like Myles had suggested, but that had turned confusing right quick. Words — or had it been a single Word? — made flesh. Turned human? Weird stuff. But Wesley would definitely keep trying.

"I am happy." Her solemn face belied her words. "But it can't be because of me." She pulled her hand out from under his, tucking both in her apron pockets.

"That doesn't even make sense. Why can't it be for you? I've never heard much about this stuff before. If it weren't for you, I wouldn't be thinking about it now. I can't change that."

"That's not completely what I meant."

Wesley raised his eyebrows. It's what she'd said. Words were words. Unless they were flesh. He shook his head. Too many kinds of odd subtext.

"What I meant was, a person needs to have a relationship with Jesus because he or she deeply desires one, not to please someone else. The only relationship is a direct one."

"O... kay."

Kass's eyes pleaded with his. If he could only make sense of what they were telling him. What her words really meant. This whole Bible thing seemed wrapped up in some encryption he didn't understand.

Was she worth cracking the code for... even when she said that wasn't a good enough reason? He couldn't deny he was drawn to it, though. It wasn't just her. Only mostly. It was Myles and Adriana, too. Marco. The whole atmosphere at Bridgeview Bible Church. He hadn't gone back every week only to see Kass or to annoy Astrid if she asked, but because there was something there. Something indefinable and alluring.

"Kass?" called Celeste.

"I need to get back to work."

Wesley nodded. "I've got four pieces in the truck to bring in and mount."

"I'll sign off on them when you're ready." She turned.

Wesley watched her lithe form walk away in her white capris and white T-shirt, with the colorful apron ties around her neck and waist. Her red-gold hair already tried to escape her ponytail.

She was amazing. He wasn't going to mess this up, even if he had to figure out how to want Jesus for himself.

CHAPTER 12

I thought I might find you here." Jasmine's words penetrated the bubble Kass had wrapped herself in down beside the river.

"Hailey blabbed."

"Maybe." Jasmine settled onto the fallen cottonwood trunk beside her. "What's up?"

Kass shook her head and shrugged at the same time.

"I hear your mom's in town."

Hailey had definitely blabbed. No surprise there. Kass had learned the hard way when they were kids. Whatever Hailey knew, the neighborhood knew. "She left my dad." Painful as the subject was, it beat talking about Wesley.

There was silence for a heartbeat or two. "I'm sorry to hear that."

"Yeah. She's been my mom since I was in first grade."

"I didn't realize she wasn't your birth mom. This is the woman I've met a couple of times, right?"

Kass nodded. "They've visited, yes. My mom died of cancer. Dad was kind of drifting when Lenore came along. She's been the glue that kept us together, really." She turned to Jasmine. "What do you do when the glue is no longer sticky?"

"I could answer that in so many ways, but let's cut through it all and get to the heart. Jesus is the only glue where the sticky never wears off. People are always going to let us down, one way or another, sooner or later. He won't."

"I know. It's just..."

The river rushed by, and a songbird trilled. Way above them, a truck rumbled over the bridge, its sound distant. Faint.

Jasmine bumped her shoulder. "Just what?"

"I've tried so hard."

"To do what, exactly?"

"To be nice. To be lovable. To not rock the boat." Why was she saying all this to Jasmine? Sure, they were friends, but no one needed to get *this* close to her.

"There seems to be a question beneath the obvious."

"Forget it." Kass stood, dusted the seat of her shorts, and pointed out into the current. "Should've brought my fly rod. Did you see that fish jump?"

"Kassidy Jane North."

She didn't turn to look at her friend. "What?"

"Talk to me. I'm all yours."

"Nothing to say."

"I don't buy that line."

"Look, I'm feeling a little vulnerable today. It will pass. Don't worry about it."

"I'm not *worried* about it. I'm your friend — one of your closest friends, besides Hailey, as far as I know. And it occurs to me that I don't really know you. What makes you tick, Kass? What are your hopes and dreams and desires?"

Wesley Ferguson.

But that was a shallow answer, and not something she was about to admit to Jasmine. It wasn't even true. She'd only met him a couple of weeks ago, and she'd been a living, breathing human before that, albeit one who'd never been passionately kissed.

"Daria told me it looked like you and Wesley had a lot to discuss after cooking club on Wednesday."

"Your sister-in-law talks too much."

"So it's true?"

"We chatted, yes. He has a cute kid."

"Way to change the subject." Jasmine angled her head. "Or are you? You told me about the guy you dated in Galena Landing. Didn't he have kids, too?"

"A lot of men do."

Jasmine grabbed Kass's hand and tugged her back down to the log. "It's true, but not that many have custody of them. Courts seem to favor the moms, even when they shouldn't. How any judge could think Catalina Romero will take better care of those kids than Vince beats me."

"She made a move on Wesley." Kass chomped down on her lip. Why had she said that? Yes, it had bugged her, but he hadn't been drawn in. On the contrary, he'd invited Kass out after that then kissed her in a way that had stirred her to her soul.

"Did she now? Figures." Jasmine leaned closer, pressing her arm against Kass's. "Still, I've known a few single dads and never once thought, wow, I should date this man and maybe marry him."

"You were in love with Nathan the whole time."

"But I didn't know he'd ever come back. That he'd have done a complete one-eighty and turned his life over to Jesus." Jasmine shook her head. "That was some kind of miracle and, even though I know God's in the miracle business, I wasn't counting on it."

God is in the miracle business. Kass knew that. But like her friend said, a person couldn't count on it. He'd performed a miracle for Nathan. Maybe they were all used up, and there weren't any left for Wesley.

"He does miracles in people's lives every day. They're not always as big and dramatic as taking a mess like Nathan had created of his life and turning it around, but they're there."

"He did it for Mason, too," Kass said quietly, remembering.

"Mason? Oh, the guy in Galena Landing? Yeah, God does it all the time. We don't always recognize it. Look at Logan Dermott for another example. God is working in people all around us." Jasmine chuckled quietly. "He did something big in me a few months ago. I might have told you."

Better to talk about Jasmine than herself, even though no doubt the story revolved around Nathan. In her friend's life these days, nearly everything did. "I don't think so?"

"I felt sometimes that my prayers were as powerful as making a wish while blowing on dandelion fluff. Basically, the words bounced off the ceiling and went nowhere."

Kass held her breath. This wasn't something Jasmine had shared before, but it sounded like what was true in her own life, too.

"My nonna reminded me that God is everywhere. Because of that, my prayers don't have to travel anywhere to reach Him. Even bounced off the ceiling is okay. I memorized Psalm 139 as a kid, but I kept forgetting about it. 'Where can I go from your Spirit? Where can I flee from your presence? If I go up to the heavens, you are there; if I make my bed in the depths, you are there. If I rise on the wings of the dawn, if I settle on the far side of the sea, even there your hand will guide me, your right hand will hold me fast.'"

Even there Your hand will guide me... "Thanks for the reminder."

"My other question needs answering, though. Why are you drawn to single dads?"

"It's better than married ones!"

"Ha ha. Very funny. Also, don't try to change the subject."

It had been a good try. "I don't know."

"How long was your father alone before Lenore came along?"

Kass swung her head and looked at her friend. "This is relevant how?" Although she should simply go with the change.

"Not sure if it is. How long?"

"About two years." Kass thought back to the little girl she'd been. She'd gone to daycare daily then kindergarten. "My dad tried, but being a parent is tough. He worked all day and still had a farm to run in his spare time. I spent a lot of hours on the tractor with him, or playing with my dolls in the shade beside a field he was haying. And he was grieving, too."

In her periphery, she caught Jasmine's nod, but Kass was in the past, inside that lonely child. She'd been so starved for love and attention that when Miss Larson began teaching her Sunday School class, she'd soaked it in like eggs on day-old bread destined for French toast. And when Dad had met this beloved teacher, all little Kassie's dreams came true.

She must have hoped history would repeat itself when she found herself teaching Mason Waterman's motherless twins in Sunday School in that same church.

Only this time, the dad attended, too. Was hungry for Jesus. Also, it turned out, hungry for a woman who was not Kass.

"I can't imagine," Jasmine said softly. "A kid needs two parents. Now that I'm a little older, I can see that parents need each other, too, to tag-team if nothing else."

Kass pushed her mind over to Jasmine's train of thought. "Lenore made a huge difference in both our lives. She showered love on me, and I adored her. My dad was still busy, but he was around more, and he laughed again. He started coming to church." Memories threatened to choke her. "I thought they were happy together."

A trout leaped from the water then disappeared with a barely discernible plop. Not even a ripple proved it had happened, not in a flowing river. So much of life was like that. Events happened, but made no difference in the grand scheme of things.

"I'm sure they were, and they probably will be again. Sometimes people need a bit of time to work through issues. I'll pray for them."

"Thanks."

"And for you to know God's will."

Kass shook her head. "I already know it."

"Oh? What's that?"

"Wesley's not a Christian, Jasmine. There can't be any happily-ever-after in that direction."

"Are you telling God what He can or can't do?

Because He's in the business of saving souls, my friend. He's brought Wesley and Sebastian into the heart of Bridgeview, parked him next door to Adriana and Myles, sent my nephew Oren as a friend for Sebastian, and piqued Wesley's interest in coming to church. Don't you think He's big enough to handle the rest?"

God was definitely big enough. But how could Kass trust anything Wesley said about God after last night? Not when Dad's interest in the church had waned over time with Lenore.

◦‿◦

"HELLO THE HOUSE!"

Wesley froze over the epoxy he'd smeared onto the edge of a broken teacup. Not that the project could wait. There was no do-over with this kind of glue. "In the backyard," he called.

Astrid strolled around the corner of the house, looking for all the world like she owned the place. She looked around the yard, braced her hands on her hips, and nodded. "So this is where the magic happens."

Was that sarcasm or heartfelt? With Astrid, it was difficult to know. The fact that he was a welder by trade had not endeared him to Sydney's intellectual parents from the beginning. No point in worrying about that now. That water was so far under the bridge it had flowed into the ocean and circled the globe a time or two.

He finished wiping the concoction down the last inch of broken china, set down the applicator, lined up the two pieces, and pressed them gently together. When he was sure the two pieces had begun bonding, he picked up the applicator and the next fragment of porcelain.

"What's that you're doing?" Astrid's voice came from over his left shoulder.

He managed not to wince away from her. "Fixing an old broken cup with kintsugi." An old mismatched teacup Sydney had left behind, but Astrid didn't need to know. Didn't know he felt an affinity with the inanimate object.

"I've heard of that. I didn't know you knew how to do it."

There were a lot of things about him that Astrid and Robert had never bothered to figure out. "I'm practicing on this piece before attempting it on an heirloom plate that was once worth thousands of dollars." He pressed the fragment against the larger piece, leaving only the two halves to go. "So far, so good."

"I'm impressed."

That required an answer? He squirted a bit more of the two-part epoxy onto his disposable tray, sprinkled in some of the gold-toned particles, and stirred it with his applicator until it was fully mixed. Then he began the task of smearing the goop as evenly as he could on the broken edge of one half.

Thankfully Astrid remained quiet, watching the process, so he could stay focused on aligning the two parts and holding them together for a couple of minutes. Then he slipped two large rubber bands around the cup to keep gentle pressure on the repair before setting it down and stripping off the disposable gloves. "What can I do for you? I need to bike over to the school and meet Sebastian in a few minutes."

Her precise eyebrows rose. "Bike?"

"Or walk, usually. It's only a few blocks. I figure I'll drive it often enough when the weather is bad in January." Not that school had been back in long enough for there to be a usually.

"We haven't seen Sebastian for over a week."

Why did he feel like he should apologize? He was the parent, not Astrid, and the bridge went both ways. "It's been busy with the first week of school and all." The *all* included Kass North. "You'll be glad to know Sebastian likes his teacher. And, because we've been going to church for a few weeks now, he already knew some of the kids. Win win."

"Good to hear. Why don't the two of you come for dinner tonight? Or, if you have plans, I can just take Sebastian home with me, and you can pick him up later."

Friday night. Usually, he would have plans. He'd like to have them tonight, but it was going to take more than a day or two to get over Kass's rejection. "Why don't you come over for Sunday lunch? We can grill."

He waved a hand toward the deck by his back door. "It's a lot easier for Sebastian here where he can play outside with his own toys."

Astrid pursed her lips, studying him.

Wesley stared back, eyebrows slightly raised.

"Fine. I'll bring a salad and dessert."

A sugar-free dessert. Well, those hadn't killed Sebastian yet, so maybe it would be okay. Wesley would claim to be too stuffed for dessert and then enjoy some butterscotch ripple ice cream after they left. Worked for him. "Thank you."

Astrid looked down at her sandals. "How far to the school? Maybe these shoes are okay, and I can walk with you. Does your school require information for other people to pick children up? If they don't, they should, but I don't remember you saying anything about putting Robert and me on the list."

Wesley forced a smile over his gritted teeth. "Good idea. If you walk up with me, we can probably get that taken care of before the final bell rings. If you're ready?"

"Your teacup will be okay like that?"

Wesley nodded. "The cat is inside and the neighbor kid is at school, so there's not much that can happen to it before it sets up." He'd already raised the latch on the side fence. No one had seemed to notice.

Astrid reached toward the cup but didn't touch. "Is that real gold?"

Of course, that's what it would come down to. "No,

it's a gold-toned mica. Fool's gold, they used to call it. But it works well mixed with epoxy to look like the real thing. It makes something beautiful out of something that was broken."

"And will the line stay bumpy like that?"

He shook his head. "There are techniques for getting it flush with the pottery once it's dried. Again, it's why I'm experimenting on something of little value."

"Would you be willing to repair a decorative plate my grandmother gave me years ago? I cried when the hook broke and it hit the floor in a dozen pieces."

This was the most civilized conversation he could ever remember having with Sydney's mother. Ten points for being on his own turf, not hers. He'd have to remember that. "I'll have a look at it, sure. By Sunday afternoon, I'll have this one finished, and you can see if it's a style you like." He stared at the golden glue oozing out of the cup's seams. "You know it won't be like new."

"I know." She touched his arm. "When something is broken, we can either leave it broken, do a haphazard job of taping it up, or make something more beautiful out of the pieces. I like what you're doing here, Wesley."

He stared at his former mother-in-law. If he wasn't mistaken, she was speaking of more than broken cups, maybe about shattered lives. "Thanks. If we want to get to the school on time, we should head out now." He ushered her toward the front of the house.

Astrid fell into step beside him. "I drove by that sweet coffee shop with the yellow and white awning on my way here. They have a Help Wanted sign in the window, and I thought maybe I'd apply for a job. Robert works long hours, and I need something to keep me busy. Wouldn't it be great if I worked right here in Bridgeview? It would be so much closer for seeing Sebastian."

Great? Wesley could think of other descriptors, like disaster. All he needed was for Astrid and Kass to meet and compare notes. "I think they already hired someone." Saved by Kass's stepmom.

"Then they should take the sign down. At any rate, it doesn't hurt to ask."

Yes. Yes, it did.

CHAPTER 13

Taking time out to sit by the river had soothed Kass's soul, at least a bit. But, when they were shorthanded at the café, she was on opening and closing both.

She swallowed the sigh and forced a smile as she pushed open the back door.

"There you are! Thank goodness." Celeste looked as frazzled as she sounded. "I'm off in five minutes and there's like twenty people having coffee and a woman just came in asking about the sign in the window."

"I told you I'd be back by four, and here I am." Kass squeezed Celeste's arm. "I hope Hailey went upstairs?"

"Yes. Shay's in the kitchen, and Lenore's pouring refills."

"Sounds good. Where's the woman who's looking for a job? I'll meet with her."

Celeste fluttered a hand toward the front of the bistro.

"I'll find her." Kass smiled. "See you in the morning."

The younger woman looked over at the bulletin board. "I might be a few minutes late."

This kept happening. Kass sucked in her breath. "You're scheduled for ten to four, because that's when we need you."

"I'll try. Saturdays are hard, when my boyfriend's home."

What it amounted to was that Celeste wanted a paycheck without actually working. And Kass needed to rethink her idea that they needed only weekday help. An extra for Saturdays would probably be a good idea. They'd gotten busier since the anniversary party. "I need you at ten, Celeste. But I promise to look for another person to work some Saturdays, okay? Then maybe you can have them off at times."

Celeste brightened. "That'd be great. Oh, look, it's four o'clock." She untied her apron. "Time to go."

Kass waved to Shay through the kitchen door, strode over to the counter, and surveyed the dining area. About ten people — all regulars — sat around, drinking coffee and swapping jokes. Plates covered with crumbs littered the tables in front of them. Coffee pot in hand, Lenore chatted with a thin woman about her own age just inside the doors. Ah, the job seeker.

"There she is now," Lenore said, beckoning to Kass.

"Hi there. I'm Kassidy North, one of the owners. How can I help you?"

"Yes. My name is Astrid Jansen. I saw your Help Wanted sign, so I thought I'd come in and see about the job you have available."

At fifty-something, this woman had to be more stable than Celeste, not that it was Celeste's replacement she was looking for... except in her dreams. "Sure, why don't we have a seat over there." Kass pointed to a table away from their late afternoon regulars. "Would you like a coffee while we chat?"

"I don't drink coffee. Green tea with stevia would be lovely."

Great. "We have green tea, but no stevia. I believe there are packets of sugar-free sweetener by the till. Lenore?"

"I'll get right on it, Kass."

Offering a cinnamon roll had been on the tip of her tongue, but they were definitely sweetened with a boatload of brown sugar. Kass kept silent as she took a seat with her back to the window so she could keep an eye on the space.

Astrid pulled out a turquoise chair across from her, and Kass looked her over. The woman was short and thin, with freckles and chin-length salt-and-pepper hair. She wore a sleeveless gray dress and clasped her hands nervously on the table between them. Heavy rings, one showcasing a large diamond, adorned several fingers.

"I'm pleased to meet you, Astrid. Do you have experience in the food service industry?"

"No."

"I see. Tell me why you'd be an asset to Bridgeview Bakery and Bistro."

Lenore set a coffee and a green tea on the table then murmured an apology for forgetting the packets.

"Oh, don't worry about it," replied Astrid. "I don't touch artificial sweeteners."

Or sugar. Or coffee. This could only get better. Right? Kass lifted her cup while she waited.

Astrid met her gaze. "My husband is an attorney working long hours, and I'm bored with my clubs. I'd like to do something more useful with my time. Also, our son-in-law and grandson moved into this neighborhood recently, and I thought it would be nice to be nearby where I could see Sebastian more often."

Perhaps the woman kept talking. Her words faded away as Kass froze. This woman was Wesley's mother-in-law? Ex-mother-in-law. Which made little difference, when the woman who'd linked them together was dead.

No. The bistro needed help — badly — but not from a woman who was bored with her rich lifestyle and was part of Wesley's circle. Astrid would be disenchanted with working after a few days or weeks and all the time spent training her would have been wasted. Kass needed someone else, but she had to remain polite.

"...his work on your walls. He's very talented."

Had Wesley sent Astrid? Would she be more invested in selling his pieces on commission than in selling coffee? Would she tell their clients sugar was bad for them? Probably.

"Yes, the art is great. Unique." But now Kass needed to get rid of Astrid without offering her a job, or any hope she'd reconsider. "This is quite a busy café, and we are looking for experienced help. There's little time for training. It's also full time, Tuesday through Saturday."

Astrid smiled at her. "I'm a quick study."

Kass took a deep breath. "We sell baked goods made with sugar. Our cinnamon rolls are very popular, and so are our cookies. And pastries. Brownies. As you don't consume sugar, I'm concerned you might find that aspect difficult."

The other woman leaned closer. "I have some terrific recipes that are sweetened with stevia and erythritol. I'd be happy to share."

"I'm afraid you don't understand. We're not looking for recipes or even kitchen help." Although, now that business was booming, Hailey might disagree. "We are looking for someone to work the counter. To make lattes, plate orders, and run the cash register. Encourage customers to try our array of baked goods. Sign them up for standing orders which usually include a weekly pickup of bread or rolls and an assortment of sweets."

Astrid nodded. "I can do that."

Kass had her doubts. Her phone rang, and she glanced at the display. Dad? "I really need to take this call."

"If there's an application, perhaps I could fill it in while you answer that."

Kass blinked as she stood. "Um, sure. Lenore, can you get a form from the clipboard under the counter?" Then she dashed out the front door to be sure her stepmom couldn't overhear the conversation. "Hi, Dad?"

FOR THE FIRST TIME, Sebastian willingly went with Oren's mom to junior church. Wesley hunkered down in his seat, already missing his little sidekick. Last week they'd said it would be Seeker Sunday, and to invite friends who were curious about Jesus. He figured he qualified, even if it was all a little peculiar.

A man strummed his guitar while a woman spoke into the microphone. Hadn't she been at the cooking club last week? "Welcome to Bridgeview Bible Church. I'm Trudy Trenton, and this is my husband, Norris." The guy nodded but didn't look up. "We're here to lead you in worship this morning. Let's stand and sing together."

Wesley rose along with everyone else.

She began to sing. "My hope is built on nothing less than Jesus' love and righteousness."

Whoa. That woman could belt it out, but everyone around him did the same. A few people hit the notes slightly off but, still, together they made quite an impact. And did they all believe those words? He watched the lyrics play across the screen at the front.

"On Christ, the solid Rock, I stand." Trudy closed her eyes and raised one hand high. "All other ground is sinking sand."

Pretty sure Christ was another name for Jesus. Wesley knew the feeling of the ground he was standing on shifting away. When Sydney had left him, taking Sebastian with her. Once again when he'd got the phone call about her accident. In fact, his entire life played out in his mind with him scrambling to find someplace where he could stand for a few months or even weeks without tilting off balance again. He'd kind of assumed it wasn't even possible. Not for him, anyway.

Norris leaned into the microphone. "When darkness veils His lovely face, I rest on His unchanging grace. In every high and stormy gale, my anchor holds within the veil."

Wesley shook his head. Words like unchanging and anchor had little meaning in his life. But he wanted them, not just for his son's sake. Sebastian had been through so much in his short life.

When that song came to a close, there was a poignant silence for a moment. It seemed Wesley wasn't the only one who needed a few seconds to think about the words that had just surrounded them.

Then Trudy nodded at Norris again, and he started playing. The guy was talented. Both of them were.

The next song asked questions about who made the world and all that was in it. The answer appeared to be the King of Glory, who demonstrated amazing, unfailing grace and love in laying down His life to set people free.

Another way to talk about Jesus again. Church wasn't as stuffy as Wesley had always thought. The people around him sang with obvious passion about God. A few of them were old, but many were in their forties, thirties, and younger.

Could Jesus be relevant? Kass thought so.

Wesley snuck a glance across the building to where she stood between her cousin and her stepmother, eyes closed and hands raised like she was having a private moment. Maybe she was.

Something stirred within him. Something that wasn't just Kass the gorgeous woman, but something deeper. Something that called to him at a cellular level.

"God, You're a good, good Father." Trudy spoke reverently. Praying, just this casually? Then she sang the same words, and the congregation joined in.

Wesley watched the lyrics cross the screen. An occasional foster dad had been decent, but none had lasted. He definitely hadn't had a father who was perfect in all of his ways. Like the lyrics said, everyone was searching far and wide. He'd experienced that. But was God — Jesus — the answer? What he needed?

Something in the depth of his soul reached toward it.

He barely noticed when Trudy and Norris exited the platform and took seats in the front.

Pastor Tomas adjusted the microphone. "Let's pray. God, we come together to worship You. To share our love for You with our friends and neighbors. I pray for every seeking heart here today, that each will see the passionate love You have for them, the lasting peace You provide, and the deep joy we find in You. Please take my words and let them be a bold invitation to eternal life with You. In the name of Your Son, Jesus, amen."

A picture of a winding dirt road popped up onto the screen, with green highway signs visible along its length.

"May I invite you to walk the Romans Road with me today?"

The screen zoomed to the first sign which said, 'all have sinned (Romans 3:23)'.

"'All have sinned and fall short of the glory of God.'" Tomas looked out at the congregation, his eyes seeming to rest on Wesley's for a long moment. "Sin is simply a word that means an offense against a divine law. Whether we've murdered someone or told a little white lie, we've all done wrong. It's hard to argue this point. 'Nobody's perfect,' we say, even when we feel we're decent people who try to do what's right."

If only Wesley could even pretend he was that good. Nope.

"The Bible tells us that God created the universe, including our natural world and humanity. Everything was perfect until sin entered the picture when Adam and Eve rebelled against God. Romans 5:12 lays out the logical progression. 'Therefore, just as sin entered the world through one man, and death through sin, and in this way death came to all people, because all sinned.'"

The pastor paused. "We can blame Eve all we want, but it doesn't change anything. Evil is here. It's present in each one of us. When Jesus walked this earth, some of the religious leaders of the day caught a woman sinning and dragged her to Jesus for sentencing. What she'd done was punishable by death in their culture, but Jesus quietly asked the one who had never sinned to be the first to throw a stone at her. The religious leaders drifted away. They couldn't do it. Even those who'd done everything right in the eyes of the law knew they'd sinned in the eyes of God."

Point one. Check. Wesley shifted in his seat.

"It gets worse before it gets better," Pastor Tomas went on. "Like in the story I mentioned, there are consequences for sin. Romans 6:23 says, 'the wages of sin is death.' God expects restitution for the wrong we've done by disobeying Him, and that's death. Separation from Him forever."

That word again, but not in a nice way. Wesley preferred the forever love picture to the forever death.

"But that verse goes on to say, 'but the gift of God is eternal life through Jesus Christ our Lord.' Now that's a big change, isn't it? From eternal death in hell — a real place, by the way, not just an unpleasant word — to eternal life in heaven — also a real place in the presence of our Creator. So how can this gift of God be given? What does Jesus have to do with it?"

The screen zoomed to yet another of the green road signs.

"This is the heart of the Bible, my friends." The pastor held up a leather-bound book. "The first two-thirds or so gives us the history of the planet and the Jewish people. How God created the earth, a bunch of stories about early people, some of whom tried to follow God. How He called Abraham into relationship with Him and promised to make a great nation from his descendants. How He built this nation and gave them the Ten Commandments and other laws, then gave them a homeland. How this nation turned their back on their God, even while some of their kings and prophets tried to caution them about the consequences of their actions."

Warnings of penalties. Wesley had tried to do that for Sydney. Others had done the same for him, but he hadn't listened. He'd kept right on his pathway, even when Sydney's journey ended abruptly... and just as badly as he'd warned her.

"But at that point in history," Tomas went on, "God came to this earth in human flesh. We celebrate Jesus' birth at Christmas time. His purpose for coming was to meet that penalty once and for all. Romans 5:8 says, 'God demonstrates his own love for us in this: while we were still sinners, Christ died for us.' Jesus was God Himself. He lived on earth for about thirty-three years and did no wrong. Then He was killed. See how that fulfills the letter of the law? The punishment — death — has been paid for all of us through God's sacrifice.

"Then we have a few verses from Romans chapter ten to wrap things up. To explain how we go from the death of Jesus, the fulfillment of the punishment, to a personal change. Listen to this. 'If you declare with your mouth, "Jesus is Lord," and believe in your heart that God raised him from the dead, you will be saved. For it is with your heart that you believe and are justified, and it is with your mouth that you profess and are saved.'"

That was it? Just saying it and believing it? It sounded too simple.

Pastor Tomas closed his Bible and rested his elbows on the podium. "That chapter goes on to say, 'Everyone who calls on the name of the Lord will be saved.' There's nothing fancy to this. It's not a convoluted weird race where only a few can find their way to the finish line. It's so simple a child can believe... and so deep an adult can. I'm not going to ask for a show of hands or invite anyone to come forward after we close. But, if you've felt the spirit of God shifting things within you today, please come talk to me or to a trusted friend. Because this message is for you."

Was it?

"You have such a beautiful home," gushed Lenore.

Kass followed her into Adriana's house as Violet and Sam charged through to the backyard. Was this where she wanted to be? Not even a little bit. Not since Wesley happened to move in next door, but she couldn't help that. Not when Adriana had come up after the closing song and invited them for lunch. Hailey had bowed out, citing a beach day with Eden and Jacob, but Mom seemed interested, so Kass hadn't felt she could turn Adriana down.

Maybe someone like Pastor Tomas and Juanita had invited him and Sebastian over for lunch. They had an open-door policy on Sundays, much like Adriana and Myles did, always prepared to welcome guests. Barring that, maybe Wesley would stay inside his house once he realized the Sheridans had guests.

One could hope.

She'd cast a surreptitious glance his way a time or two during Tomas's sermon, and Wesley had seemed totally absorbed. She should have been happy about that. She *was* happy. It was just that she didn't trust his motives. Did that make her a horrible person?

"Thank you. I'm blessed in so many ways." Adriana's eyes met Myles's.

Another reminder that so many of her friends had found love. Aargh. Where was Kass's cynicism coming from? She was happy for Adriana and Myles. She was.

"Come on in the kitchen," invited Adriana. "It's just a simple lunch today. My parents visited from Arcadia Valley recently and brought me a cooler full of Delis sausages, so Myles will light the grill. I could use a hand finishing off the salads I have prepped and taking them out to the deck."

The deck where Kass would have a perfect view through the fence to Wesley's backyard. Nice. But it wasn't all about her. She needed to get Lenore's mind off Dad for a couple of hours.

"Are you visiting here for long?" Adriana asked.

Lenore glanced at Kass. "A few weeks. I'm helping out at the bistro until Ava, I think her name is, is back to work."

"That's so sweet of you. I'm sure Kass and Hailey appreciate you a lot. It's good of your husband to spare you for that long."

About that. Dad had flipped a switch when he

found out his wife had come to Spokane and Kass
hadn't told him. He'd ordered Lenore home immedi-
ately, but she held her ground. There had been many
tears afterward while Lenore tried to get Kass's opinion
of her refusal.

No way was Kass getting involved more than she
had to. Providing refuge was complicit enough.

"He'll be fine. It's probably good for us to be apart
for a bit."

Adriana lifted a questioning brow. She didn't have
to challenge Lenore for Kass to know she wanted to.
No doubt newlyweds like Adriana and Myles couldn't
imagine anything less than perfect love.

Only Jesus loved perfectly. Kass would do well to
remember Pastor Tomas's sermon herself. It hadn't just
been targeted at the likes of Wesley.

"Mom!" yelled Violet. "That cat is in our yard
again."

Adriana rolled her eyes. "She's absolutely obsessed
with the cat next door. If Violet has rules, animals
should, too." She turned toward the French doors. "It's
okay, sweetie. Taz isn't hurting anything."

"He's looking at the chickens."

"It's fine."

Myles's deeper voice kicked in, and Adriana turned
back to the kitchen. "Sorry about that. She's convinced
Taz is up to no good. She's the only one who cares.
Duke and the chickens certainly don't. I found the cat
curled up in Sam's lap yesterday while he read in the

hammock, so he's happy enough to have a part-time pet." She shook her head. "I don't know what goes through Violet's head some days."

Kass smiled. "She's a unique one." There wasn't much else to say, really. If every person marched to the beat of their own drummer, Violet had invented her own personal percussion band. A different beat wasn't enough for that one.

"Kass, can I get you to toss the Caesar salad and take it out to the deck?" Adriana set a bowl and a jar full of dressing onto the kitchen island.

"Sure can."

"And Lenore, if you could mix this quinoa salad, that would be great." She pulled more fixings out of the fridge.

"I'd love to."

Kass finished prepping the salad and took it outside, where Myles stood adjusting the heat on the large grill. Sam leaned on the table near his stepdad.

Myles grinned at her. "Thanks, Kass. Adriana and I appreciate your friendship."

"Dad!" whined Violet. "Sassy pecked at the cat."

Sam turned to his younger sister. "Is Taz bleeding?"

"Not yet."

"Then it's not a problem."

Myles chuckled. "Your mother taught you well when to bother a grownup and when not to."

Sam grinned at Myles. "Violet's a drama queen."

Kass looked over to where Violet crouched mere

inches from Sebastian's gray cat. The flock of hens pecked in the ground several feet away. Beyond the fence, Sebastian ran down the back stairs of the house next door.

She turned to face Myles again. "Is there anything I can do out here?"

"Other than put the cat through the gate, no."

"I... are you serious? Because won't it just come back any time it wants to?"

He sighed, chuckling. "It will, yes. But it might take a while, and it might save the peace meanwhile." He glanced over. "Oh, there's Sebastian. He'd take the cat from you."

Myles was serious. How could Kass say no, after she'd offered to help? She couldn't. "Okay, fine." Kass marched down the steps and across the lawn then scooped up the furry cat, who began to purr.

"What are you going to do?" Eyes bright, Violet popped up beside Kass.

"Give the cat to Sebastian."

"Can you reach the latch? Because I can't." The little girl dashed ahead and pointed upward. "See? I used to be able to, but *he* moved it. He doesn't like me." She plopped her hands on her hips and glared through the fence.

Voices came from inside Wesley's house, growing louder.

"Hey, Sebastian, here's your cat." Kass scanned the tall gate, but couldn't see a latch on this side at all.

There'd been one a few weeks ago, hadn't there? Oh, wait. It was high on the other side. She could barely reach it by threading her hand through the metal supports. Looked like Violet was right.

A person could hardly blame Wesley, though. Living next door to a free-range Violet would be a trial Kass couldn't wish on anyone.

Violet rushed through as soon as the gate opened. "Hi, little boy. We brought your cat home. He keeps getting in our yard. Our dog is going to eat him."

Sebastian stared with wide eyes from Violet to his pet to Violet.

Kass held out the cat, and the boy grabbed the furry beast, clutching it to his chest. "D-don't let him."

The door began to open.

Kass grabbed Violet's hand and towed her to the open gate, where Duke stood peering into the neighboring yard. "Come on."

"I don't want to," objected Violet, digging in her heels.

"Lunch is ready at your house." Kass pushed the child through the gate and clicked it shut.

Violet glared at her. "That wasn't very nice."

Kass crouched. "Our job was to give the cat back, not hang around and be a nuisance. We accomplished our goal." She didn't want to look back, but somehow, she couldn't help herself.

Wesley stood a few feet away, his hand on Sebastian's shoulder, watching her with a strange expression on his face. And not far behind him stood Astrid and a man who could only be Astrid's husband.

❧

"WHAT HAPPENED?" Wesley asked, tilting Sebastian's face upward.

His son held up Taz, who jumped down and strolled away, tail straight up. Wesley could only hope Taz wasn't headed for a return trip this quickly.

"Isn't that the young woman from the bistro?" asked Astrid.

Two people he'd hoped to keep apart. Wesley turned toward his former in-laws. "Yes. Kass North. She's friends with my neighbors. I've seen her there before." And other places he didn't want to talk about, like down by the river not many steps away, tucked in his arms.

"Sh-she's nice." Then Sebastian shook his head earnestly. "N-not V-Violet."

"I stopped by on Friday," Astrid went on. "I filled in an application, but I don't think she liked me. I'm not sure why."

Let him think. How many ways could Wesley count where Astrid might make a poor first impression?

"Even telling her the artist was my son-in-law made no difference."

That would have been the only strike against Astrid that Kass would need.

Astrid frowned. "She said they needed someone with experience. How much could possibly be required? The other woman poured coffee and smiled at people. I can certainly do that."

Wesley glanced over as Kass stood, took Violet's hand, and walked her back to the Sheridans' deck, where Adriana and Lenore had just come outside.

"That's the other woman right there."

"Lenore is Kass's mom." No little white lies. "Her stepmom, that is."

"Astrid, this idea of you getting a job is utter nonsense. I provide plenty well for you."

Go, Robert.

"I have too much time on my hands."

That was true.

"There are plenty of places to volunteer, like some of the environmental causes or the library. Maybe even at Sebastian's school."

Astrid brightened. "Oh, that's a good idea."

Or not. "I drove by a thrift shop the other day and saw a Help Wanted sign."

Robert shook his head. "Too dangerous. All kinds of people go into places like that."

"Just people who need a helping hand," Wesley replied.

"Not a good fit for Astrid."

Sydney's mom turned to watch what was happening in the yard next door as everyone gathered around the table, held hands, and bowed their heads. "Are they praying?"

She made it sound like the most ridiculous thing in the world. "It's called saying grace, Astrid. People pray to thank God for the food they have. When you consider the plight of so many on this planet, we really shouldn't forget our blessings."

She swung to face him. "You're starting to sound like one of them. You've been going to that church for how long now? It's quite enough."

"A few weeks." Wesley refused to break eye contact. "I kind of like it. Pastor Tomas makes a guy think, and there's great music. You should come check it out sometime."

Astrid's mouth opened and closed. "Robert. Do something."

Robert shrugged. "He's a grownup, and not even our child to start with. We can't make him do anything. Plenty of good people go to church. Doesn't hurt them any."

"But our grandson..."

"There are lots of kids his age. He really likes it." Wesley ruffled his son's hair. "Don't you, buddy?"

Sebastian nodded. "Oren's there. An-and Tieri, and J-Jack, and Manny."

Oren was Marco and Daria's, and Manny was one of the pastor's kids. Wesley didn't even know the others. He grinned at Astrid. "See? Lots of kids. It's good for him."

He turned to look inside the heated grill beside the back deck. He'd checked the frozen meals from cooking club after Astrid left on Friday and, thankfully, discovered two quinoa-and-cheese casseroles. There were also marinated chicken breasts. Sounded like food Astrid would eat, so he'd taken them all out last night and put the casseroles in the grill just before Astrid and Robert had arrived. He could only hope she hadn't gone completely vegetarian since he'd last noticed.

"So what are you cooking us?" She leaned around his elbow.

Why had he never realized why the little girl from next door annoyed him so much? She reminded him of Astrid. He could thank his lucky stars he'd been smart enough to buy a house halfway across the city from Sydney's parents. Or he could thank God. In the light of the past few weeks, that might be more to the point.

"I think I told you about the cooking club I joined?"

Astrid frowned. "No?"

Could he do this without mentioning Kass's name again? "I saw a brochure at a local business and signed up. A bunch of people get together once a month at the community center over by the bridge and prep a whole pile of meals together, then everyone takes home packages for the freezer. Sebastian and I went last week, before school started up. Our first station was garlic bread, and then we switched to marinade." He opened one of the bags of chicken and pulled out a breast with his tongs. "And here's part of the result. I think it will be a great help for keeping us in good healthy food."

Astrid eyed the bag. "What kind of marinade?"

"Uh... teriyaki. Homemade."

"Does that have sugar in it?"

Oh, boy. Why hadn't he thought of that? "It sure does. Sorry. I can rinse off one of the pieces if you prefer."

She rolled her eyes. "Never mind. I guess a few grains of the white death won't kill me."

"Probably not."

She sniffed. "I think that bakery needs me."

Uh oh. Wesley arranged the four chicken breasts on the grill. "Why's that?"

"Everything has sugar. You can smell it in the air."

He'd noticed. Mighty tantalizing, mingling with chocolate and cinnamon and ginger and yeast. "Tell me you didn't offer to overhaul their menu."

"Not exactly."

Where was Robert, anyway? Wesley glanced around to see Robert sitting beside Sebastian on the back step, chatting quietly. He was on his own. "Look, you can't just go around telling people, especially businesses, that they're evil for eating sugar."

"I didn't use the word evil."

"Astrid." He stared at her, tongs in his hand.

She lifted both hands. "Nobody ever wants to hear the truth. They'd all rather go to hell in a hand-basket gorging on sugar and corn syrup. Corn syrup is banned in Europe, yet nearly everything in America is full of it. Did you know that?"

Wesley slapped the lid of the grill shut. She didn't know how close she was to the truth... and yet how far. What would she have thought of Tomas's sermon this morning? Everyone was going to hell in a hand-basket, all right, but not because of sweets. Because of sin disguised as carefree fun. It had taken Sydney, and Wesley could feel the pull of it even now.

He'd have taken a few minutes to talk to Tomas after church if he hadn't needed to hurry home before the Jansens arrived. But at least Myles was right next door. One or the other would be happy to answer Wesley's questions as soon as there was a little time.

our friends are nice," Lenore commented as she and Kass walked back to the apartment.

It *had* been pleasant, at least once Kass had settled in a deck chair with her back to Wesley's yard. "Adriana loves to entertain. She's even begun hosting some paid dinners, like a pop-up restaurant in a private home. She'd planned to do more of that, but Myles entered her life over the winter and rather distracted her."

Her stepmom smiled. "They seem happy together."

Kass wouldn't have noticed the wistfulness if she hadn't glanced over to see the dampness in Lenore's eyes. "They are."

"I should have done things so differently, but if I had, I'd have missed out on the very best relationship I've ever had — being your mom."

Tears flooded Kass's eyes. "I'm so thankful for you."

She couldn't block the vision of motherless Sebastian, a child who deserved a mom, just as six-year-old Kass had. "I don't know how Dad and I would have fared without you."

They rounded the last intersection, and the side of Bridgeview Bakery and Bistro came into view, the yellow-and-white awning wrapping the corner.

Lenore jerked to a stop. "Speaking of which."

Dad's half-rusted pickup sat at the curb, with his tanned elbow protruding from the lowered window.

Kass checked her phone, but he hadn't called. Not his daughter, at least. Maybe after talking to Lenore on Friday night, he'd been worried she'd disappear again if he told her he was coming.

Lenore ran down the sidewalk, sandals flapping against the cement. "Farrell!"

The pickup door creaked open, and Dad emerged in faded jeans, a short-sleeved plaid shirt, and a baseball cap. A second later, Lenore slammed into his arms, nearly knocking him over. They stood, clutching each other and rocking, and Kass's mind careened back to Thursday night in Wesley's arms. She'd had no business being there, not when they weren't going the same direction, but she hadn't known that at the moment. Life had seemed full of hope, full of promise, for a blissful little while.

Kass stayed rooted to the spot. It felt like an intimate moment she shouldn't be observing, yet it wasn't. Maybe her parents would be okay, after all. Maybe Dad had realized the treasure he had in Lenore. Maybe Kass should disappear around the corner again. Give them a bit of time while she wrestled about Wesley before God.

Her parents pulled apart slightly and looked her way. Lenore held out one hand toward Kass.

No. She didn't want to interfere, but her feet started down the hill anyway. She stepped into the family circle and felt secure with all three of them holding each other close. After a moment, she peered up at her dad. "So... is everything okay?"

Dad looked at Lenore. "Up to your stepmother. If she'll come home today, everything's fine. Forgive and forget."

Lenore's chin tipped up. "I'm not going back right now. We still have things to work through and, besides, I promised Kass and Hailey to help out in the bistro until their other worker returns in a few weeks."

Her dad shook his head, his eyes narrowing. "That's not the message you sent me, running when you saw me."

Kass really, really didn't want to listen to this, but the arms surrounding her stayed in place.

"Farrell, I love you." Lenore kissed Dad's cheek. "I always will. Nothing has changed in that regard. But the reasons I left are valid until they're not. I feel like we need some time apart. Maybe some counseling to make our marriage the best it can be."

"There's nothing wrong with our marriage."

Uh oh. Those were fighting words, but Lenore just smiled and shook her head. "I disagree. I love you enough to want the very best. Do you love me that much?"

"You putting me on the spot, woman?"

She lifted a shoulder and dropped it. "Either you do or you don't."

"Of course I love you."

"Then work with me." She turned to Kass. "Do you know of any marriage counselors around here?"

"You expect me to make this drive every week?" Dad protested. "Come home, and we'll discuss it there."

"At home, there's the farm and chores and day jobs and clubs and all the other everyday things. So, no."

"You can't mean this, Lenore. We love each other. What's the big deal?"

Kass pushed out of the intimate circle. "Why don't the two of you go upstairs? Hailey's away for the day, and I'm going for a walk for, say, an hour or two. There's pop and iced tea in the fridge, so help yourself. Dad, you're welcome to stay for supper."

"But..." Dad glowered.

"I'll be back in a while." Kass backed up a few steps.

"Just a sec." Lenore held out her hand. "Kass, does your pastor do marriage counseling?"

Dad shook his head, his lips tight and face grim.

"I know he has a degree in counseling, but I'm not sure if it covers marriage, specifically." Although Pastor

Tomas offered pre-marital sessions to the couples he married. "You could give him a call and ask. His number is in the church directory on the office desk."

"Thanks. I'll do that. If he doesn't feel he can handle it, he might have someone to suggest."

"Good idea." Kass backed up a few more steps. Where was she going to spend the next couple of hours? Not back at Adriana's, next door to Wesley. Jasmine was no doubt up at Nathan's house. Hailey, Eden, and Jacob had gone to the beach for the day. Who did that leave? But she didn't want to talk to anyone, not after a couple of hours with people all around at church and then Adriana's. This was her day off. She needed silence. The river?

Or maybe the community garden, just a couple of blocks over. There might be a few neighbors there, weeding or harvesting, but there was always the gazebo or one of the benches tucked into a corner. A place where she could watch the bees, birds, or butterflies and recenter herself.

A few minutes later she opened the gate in the white picket fence. The solar fountain burbled quietly, and the fragrance from long banks of herbs and flowers permeated the air. Kass inhaled deeply and waved to the middle aged couple picking tomatoes in one of the raised beds.

The herb bed was the farthest from them and had a few weeds poking out amid the sorrel. Kass knelt to pluck the offenders.

"Kassidy North."

Had she looked like she wanted to be disturbed? She found a smile and looked up at Jasmine's grandmother. "Good afternoon, Marietta. How are you doing these days?"

"I am well." The older woman waved toward the yard next door. "So long as my girls are able to make ratatouille soon before the eggplants grow bitter. They are so busy with their own things, they forget to help an old woman out."

"Everyone is busy, that's true." Kass wouldn't bother mentioning that Marietta demanded help her daughters-in-law and granddaughters had not offered. Sure, helping out family was a positive, but Jasmine had commented that her nonna had sent her to the store for canning jars, which meant she had more than two hundred full ones in her pantry. It wasn't as though Marietta — or anyone in the Santoro family — was going to go hungry in the next five years.

Marietta harrumphed as she bent to pinch blooms off a basil plant.

"If you have vine-ripened tomatoes for sale, I'd be happy to buy some for the bistro. We're going through a lot of gazpacho at lunchtimes with the weather so hot, and lots of our regular customers love when we have vine-ripened tomatoes for sandwiches."

"And then what would I do with the eggplants?" Marietta glared at her, as though any imbalance would be completely Kass's fault.

"I could buy those, as well." Kass's mind sped to flavorful baba ganoush. "The ones Jasmine and Peter are growing in the Johnsons' yard got dug up by their new puppy, so Bridgeview Backyards hasn't been able to fill my order."

"Jasmine keeps trying to sell my produce," grumbled Marietta.

"Only if you have extra."

The older woman sighed. "Come tomorrow and we will see what we can do."

Kass nodded. "I'll be happy to. Is morning better, or afternoon?"

"Morning."

"Sure. I'll do that." Did she dare interfere about other matters? Oh, why not. "Have you had anyone look at the empty rental on Water Street?"

Marietta shot her a daggered look. "Only the Ranta boy and a few other misfits. I'll place another ad in the Spokesman-Review next week."

"Dan is hardly a boy. Hailey went to school with him, so he must be nearly thirty."

"Living with a tramp not his wife and a pile of kids. I don't want anyone to think I condone that kind of lifestyle."

To say nothing of how Dixie had been in the car with Marietta's grandson Basil the night he'd run an alcohol checkpoint a few months back. "Dan's been asking a lot of questions about Jesus. Wouldn't it be neat if he decided to give his life to the Lord?"

"God is in the redeeming business, but I'm not sure that man is a good candidate."

"Why not? Sounds like God's already at work." And why should Kass think Dan could make that sort of lifechanging decision, but not Wesley? Dan stood to lose Dixie and the kids if he did, while Wesley stood to gain Kass. No. She wasn't going to think about it that way.

"I guess it can't hurt to pray."

"True enough. I know Eden and Jacob have been praying for their new neighbors, whoever they might be. They're hoping it's someone where they can make a difference in their life."

Marietta's hand stilled, but Kass didn't look up. Feeling the pointed stare like a needle stabbing her cheek was enough. "You think I should let them live in sin in my house?"

"I didn't say that. Whom you lease to is entirely up to you."

"He probably makes enough money with his landscaping business to pay the rent. He's a hard worker."

"I've heard he is. Trying to make some changes with more environmentally sound practices now that he's in charge. Linnea told me he lost a few clients but gained others, so I think it evened out. Plus he's been working on a marketing plan with Nathan."

Marietta grunted.

Kass hadn't found the peace she'd been looking for in the garden, but she'd found some fresh produce for the bistro and may have done a good turn for Dan Ranta, so she'd have to consider it time well spent, anyhow.

Maybe a walk along the river would be more restful.

WITH THE DINOSAURS shipped off to their new home, Wesley eyed the Tuscan Works plate on his workbench a few days later. It was in about a dozen pieces, with gaps where the fragments had been too small to handle. The gold-infused epoxy would fill those.

He glanced at the shelf where the teacup and an old bowl sat, golden lines outlining the breaks. They were whole again. Not food-grade worthy, but even more precious. Works of art, really. Would people pay for such things?

Why not? They paid good money for owls and dinosaurs made from rusted machine parts. Why not from broken pottery?

His fingers traced the gold filigree in the heirloom plate. Whole and unbroken, this would have brought a small fortune at auction, but it could be beautiful again. Shattered objects didn't have to be garbage. Discarded. Worthless.

The irony was not lost.

He laid out a new work surface then mixed enough epoxy to begin reassembling the plate. This phase couldn't be rushed. He couldn't simply stick all the bits together and voila, finished. No, it had to be done two pieces at a time, with care, allowing each to align and bond before adding the next section. Moving too quickly would only result in something askew, something that would still be trash, only larger than it had been before.

No one needed bigger junk.

And a man couldn't erase his past. The mess was there, a permanent part of who he was. Now Jesus... Wesley was starting to think this Man could perform kintsugi on people's lives. Take the garbage and make something far more beautiful than the sum of its parts warranted.

Could God take a messed-up foster kid who'd tried to make something of himself — and failed — and create a masterpiece?

The book of John was full of stories about healing, so far. Other stories Wesley had read several times this week and failed to understand, but they called to him, whispering promises of peace and satisfaction.

Would that they were true.

CHAPTER 16

Sirens shrieked as a police car squealed by. Seconds later an ambulance followed, lights flashing, siren blaring.

Kass stared out the bistro window, heart in her mouth, hand across her chest. Who was it? What had happened? Bridgeview wasn't on an easy through-road to any other part of Spokane, tucked under the bridge as it was. So that meant the emergency vehicles' destination lay within the neighborhood.

The sirens cut off no more than a few blocks away, the silence as deafening as the sound had been.

Neighbors who, seconds before, had been laughing with friends over afternoon coffee and cookies, elbowed each other out the door in their haste to see what had happened. Some stood on the sidewalk, peering west, while others dashed behind the vehicles.

Mom and Hailey stepped up on either side of Kass.

"Did you see what happened?" Hailey cast a worried frown out the open door. "Where did they go?"

Kass shook her head. "No idea. I don't smell smoke."

"There wasn't a fire truck, anyway."

Also true. Police plus ambulance. Accident? But where?

"Maybe someone had a heart attack. Like possibly Marietta." Hailey raised her eyebrows at Kass.

"Then why the police?"

"Right." Hailey rushed out the door and joined the speculating customers gathered on the sidewalk.

Lenore tugged Kass's arm. "We need to pray." She launched into a heartfelt plea for the unknown emergency and those caught up in it.

"Could I get a refill over here?"

Oh, no. Kass pivoted. She'd thought everyone had left the building, but an older man, a stranger, had been seated alone beyond the group of thirty-somethings on break.

Lenore looked at her hands as though surprised she wasn't holding the coffee pot. "Be right there."

"No rush."

Kass surveyed the messy — and nearly vacant — dining room as her stepmother carried the carafe over. Would all these patrons be back, or would they forget where they'd been and what they'd been doing when disaster struck?

What kind of tragedy had it been? Kass breathed another prayer as she straightened chairs and picked up empty plates. Her only local family members had been in the bistro with her, so Hailey and Lenore were safe. But there weren't many residents of Bridgeview she didn't at least recognize on sight. The worry lay heavily on her heart.

A timer buzzed in the back, but Hailey wasn't in sight. Kass dashed past the counter into the kitchen. Something in the oven, maybe? Yes, the peppermint chocolate cookies in the second oven looked perfect, so she pulled them out.

Hailey hurried in the door. "Sorry. I've got those." She snagged the next pan and began to transfer the aromatic rounds to a cooling rack.

"Could you see anything?"

Her cousin shook her head. "Someone said the ambulance had gone up the hill at the end of the street, not down, so the emergency isn't likely to be at Eden's or Adriana's."

Or at Wesley's, since he also lived close to the river. Kass dared to breathe, but the heavy foreboding barely lifted. The crisis was still almost certainly with someone she knew. Maybe even at the school. *Please, Lord, not a child.*

Behind her, chatter increased as patrons returned to their seats. "I need to get out to the front. I'll let you know if I hear anything."

"Please." Hailey bit her lip as she looked up. "I'm so worried."

"Me, too. I'm glad I know you and Lenore are okay."

"Your dad isn't coming into the city today, is he?"

Kass shook her head even as another panic spiked. They hadn't expected him Sunday, either. But he wouldn't have continued west through Bridgeview. "No, their counseling sessions will be on Thursday evenings."

"Good." Hailey scooped more cookie batter onto the trays.

Yes, it was good. Dad was grumbling and whining all the way, but he'd caved once he realized Lenore wasn't returning home if he didn't. Their marriage was a worry for another day.

"Where's Celeste?" Kass asked her stepmother.

Lenore shook her head. "Said she had to go home and left."

"Oh, good grief. She knows we're shorthanded so I don't dare fire her. But it is oh, so, tempting."

"Give her a little grace and love. I think she'll come around."

"I've given her a lot of leeway, Mom. Seriously."

"Aren't you glad God's grace never gives up on us?" Lenore patted Kass's arm and turned toward the counter as a customer approached.

Kass stared at her stepmom, always so positive even with her marriage on precarious ground. Her belief in

God seemed unshakeable. Now if only Kass could learn to trust as wholeheartedly.

Starting with the current emergency.

THE AMBULANCE CAREENED the other way — toward the elementary school — at the end of the street. Wesley stood riveted in his front yard, hand on his bicycle seat. Classes would be out in fifteen minutes. Had some disaster struck at the playground? A child injured, maybe? Please, God, not Sebastian.

"Did you see where it went?" Adriana's pinched voice came from behind him.

"Turned right at the top of the hill." He turned to face her.

"The school?" Her face was pale, her eyes wide, her hands trembling.

"That direction, anyway. But there are lots of houses in that area, too."

Her hands clenched in front of her face. "No. Please, no."

Right. Her husband was a teacher at Bridgeview Elementary, both kids students. "I'm sure it's not the school, Adriana. They'd have let us know by now, don't you think? You, for sure."

"My late husband was a firefighter." Her voice was faint.

What could Wesley say to that? It likely wouldn't

comfort her to be reminded a ladder truck hadn't been in today's mix.

"He died in the line of duty. I even heard the sirens that night, but didn't know he was personally in danger. I mean, more danger than usual. He'd gone back in to carry an old woman out of the blaze."

"I'm sorry."

She blinked, shaking her head. "Every time I hear emergency vehicles, I get thrown back into that memory. And then last winter, the sirens were for Violet."

A story Wesley hadn't heard before. "What happened?"

"She fell in the river. In February. It was freezing and very high. She was trying to save the dog."

"Save the dog?" repeated Wesley. That didn't even make sense. Duke weighed three or four times what Violet did.

"It was terrible." Adriana covered her face with her hands. "Every time I hear sirens, I remember the fear, the panic."

"But she was okay." Unlike Adriana's late husband. Way to put a foot in it.

She took a deep, shuddering breath. "Yes."

"Look, I planned to ride up to the school to meet Sebastian. I can walk instead, if you want to walk with me. We can see for ourselves in just a couple of minutes."

Adriana met his gaze for the first time. "Would you mind?"

"Not at all." He leaned the bike against the side of the carport, unbuckled his helmet, and hooked it over the handlebar. "Let's go."

She fell into step beside him, still looking as nervous as all get out.

"Who lives here?" Wesley pointed at a red brick house as they rounded the corner. "I haven't met all the neighbors yet."

"Brian and Nancy Robertson. They own a boutique downtown."

"And the house next door?"

Adriana filled him in on the neighbors, house by house. Her voice steadied as her pace picked up. Soon, they turned at the next corner, with Bridgeview Elementary in view straight ahead. No emergency vehicles were in sight. Kids played in the playground. Cars queued up at the curb like any other day, although the drivers stood huddled in little groups angling down the street.

Wesley heaved a large sigh of relief. Out loud, partly for Adriana's benefit. "See? Our families are fine."

A small sob escaped her throat. "But someone's isn't." She broke into a run.

Didn't tragedies happen every day, even within this city? Accidents, illnesses, overdoses, deaths. It wasn't that he was callused, but a man couldn't mourn for everybody. Or was it just that he hadn't ever immersed himself in a community like Adriana had?

Ahead of him, she jolted to a stop as she reached the crosswalk then hurried across, gaze fixed west. Could the accident scene — if that's what it was — be visible? Wesley put on a burst of speed of his own.

⌒⌒

KASS'S PHONE buzzed with an incoming text. She paused in the middle of a crowded but subdued bistro. Normally she wouldn't even look, as busy as it was, but chatter eased as the patrons at nearby tables turned to look at her. They were all curious, too. No, more than curious. Concerned.

She flashed a smile and removed a few plates then carried them to the kitchen. Once out of sight of prying eyes, she leaned against a wall and flicked open her cell.

Jasmine. *Please pray for my Uncle Al. He was in an accident and it's not looking good. They're taking him to Deaconess.*

Kass inhaled sharply. Alberto Santoro was the youngest of Marietta's five sons and the father of five of his own kids... the youngest, Michael, still in elementary school. Al's wife, Winnie, helped out with the cooking club and other community initiatives, always with a smile.

She tapped back. *Will def pray. Bistro is full of people who saw the ambulance go by. May I share?*

Yes. Details later.

Kass debated her next response but had only typed *k* when Hailey interrupted her thoughts. "What's going on?"

"That was Jasmine. Al Santoro was in an accident. Jasmine says it's not looking good and they're taking him to Deaconess Hospital." She took a deep breath. "She's asking for prayer."

Hailey sucked in her lip. "No other details?"

Kass shook her head. "That's it for now. I'm going to make an announcement." She thumbed toward the eating area. "Jasmine said to go ahead and let people know."

A timer buzzed and Hailey turned away, dashing moisture from her eyes.

Kass knew how she felt. Business carried on, no matter that disaster struck a close friend's family. She squared her shoulders and returned to the dining room. The quiet discussions shut off completely as everyone turned to look at her. Somehow, they knew.

"Al Santoro was in an accident, and the family is asking for prayer. He's being taken to Deaconess."

"Was that the ambulance we heard?" someone called out.

"Probably." It hadn't even crossed Kass's mind that there could have been more than one call-out. Al was an arborist who worked all over the city. "I don't know where, exactly, this accident was."

"Will he be okay?" asked another patron.

It doesn't look good. What did that even mean?

"They wouldn't ask for prayer if it weren't serious," said someone else.

Kass nodded. "So true. I'm not sure when we'll hear more, but please do keep the Santoro family in your prayers." An idea took hold. "I'll make a sign-up sheet and put it at the counter for anyone who wants to take meals to the family. I'm sure Winnie will appreciate not having to worry about feeding her crew for the next few days."

"I'll take them supper tomorrow," called Rebekah Roper.

"I've got the next day!" hollered someone further back.

This was the Bridgeview Kass knew and loved. "I'll get a paper right now." When she'd set it on the counter, neighbors crowded around, jostling for the pen. Kass couldn't help grinning. By the looks of it, Winnie wouldn't have to cook for a month.

If only it wouldn't be needed for more than a day or two. *God? Would you please heal Al in a show of Your power, so all can see and rejoice with the Santoros?*

All... like Wesley, who wasn't even sure God existed. She'd been trying to block thoughts of him and the heart-stopping kiss that should never have happened. She'd been trying to keep focused and busy, but nothing seemed to stop her thoughts from drifting to Wesley and his small son frequently throughout the packed days and empty nights.

It seemed so self-serving to pray for Wesley's salvation and, yet, how could she not? Wasn't he a lost child loved by God? Didn't the eternal Father extend His open arms to Wesley, inviting him to be His child? And so she prayed.

CHAPTER 17

A hushed atmosphere still lay over Bridgeview hours later. Even Wesley, a newcomer, felt it. He couldn't help glancing at the sky frequently — the aura of impending doom lay as heavily as that one tornado warning in Oregon a few years back, when the power was out and the sky a weird greenish-yellow color beneath the weighty dark cloud. He'd been far enough inland not to experience the full effects of that storm, but his memories of the ambience were at least as strong as that of the sky.

Today felt similar, except the sky was clear and blue, perfect for early September, with a few puffy white clouds drifting high above. Birds still sang, planes still descended overhead toward Spokane's international airport, traffic still rumbled across the bridge a couple of blocks away.

For some reason, he couldn't stay inside, but even

out in his shop, he couldn't focus on his projects. Just as well, since he didn't like having Sebastian around the equipment, and his child was as affected as he was.

"Daddy, that b-boy was crying. B-but he's a big boy." Not the first time Sebastian had mentioned this.

"Even big boys cry sometimes." Wesley had seen the principal, Ms. Philson, leaning toward a dark-haired sixth-grader. A Santoro boy, son of the man who'd been loaded into the ambulance not two blocks down. With wood chips and leaves spread for twenty feet down the street, it wasn't like the boy hadn't recognized the smashed remains of his dad's work truck.

Wesley's gut still clenched at the memory of the boy's face. At least Sebastian had been spared the sight of Sydney's car and mangled body. This boy — Michael, Adriana said — would no doubt relive the sight for years to come.

"Come on over for coffee?" Myles's voice came from beyond the fence.

Wesley turned and took a few steps closer. "Any news?"

"Not much. Al hasn't regained consciousness since surgery."

"That's rough."

Sebastian's hand snuggled into his. The thought of his own son losing his daddy was too much to bear.

"It really is. The whole community is praying for him. Praying for Winnie and the kids. Their eldest is in college in Seattle. He'll be driving in tonight."

"Praying? That's great, but isn't it up to the doctors?"

"God has granted knowledge and skills to medical professionals, for sure." Myles studied him. "But God is in control. He's the Alpha and Omega, the beginning and the end. He sees everything and has all the power in the universe at His disposal. Believe me, He could snap His fingers — figuratively, of course — and Al would leap off that gurney in ICU, completely healed."

Talk about faith. Wesley stared. "Do you really believe that will happen? Because... it just doesn't."

"I believe it *could* happen. Not that it *will*, necessarily. But if we don't ask God, why would He intervene? The Bible tells us to bring our burdens to God because He cares for us, to pray without ceasing, to believe in His power."

"But..." He glanced down at his young son. Sebastian eagerly shared what the lessons had been in junior church every week. Wesley didn't want to squelch the kid's faith but, at the same time, was it just a fairytale? The meteor the other night seemed to announce God's reality and presence, but he'd seen many meteors over his lifetime. And while Pastor Tomas's words clung to Wesley's soul, where was the proof?

"Been reading in John?"

Wesley blinked. It was like his neighbor read his mind. "Some, yeah. It's weird. So many metaphors or whatever you call them. I was never very good at figuring those out in school."

"I believe those are there to make us think. We turn them over and over in our minds, like trying to solve a Rubik's cube."

"I was never good at those, either."

Myles chuckled. "Same for me. My younger brother excelled at them. He went on to code video games for a living, so I guess there's a certain kind of unique brain there. But thinking is always good. It's what makes us human."

It was true that the stories he'd read churned in Wesley's mind. What did they mean? He'd heard the term *born again* spoken derogatorily more often than positively, but there it was in the Bible as though it was a real thing. *No one can see the kingdom of God unless they are born again.*

Was the kingdom of God the same as heaven? Both seemed somehow wrapped up in the forever thing Kass had talked about. Life after death. Because surely the kingdom of God couldn't be here, right now. Not with all the mess in the world, evidenced by a well-loved father, husband, and church-goer lying unresponsive in the hospital. Yet something surrounded that man. A loving family that Wesley could only dream about, and more. An entire community talking in hushed tones, walking on pins and needles, waiting for news.

Praying while they waited.

"About coffee?" Myles asked again. "Adriana's baking up a storm, enough to supply the entire Santoro clan for days to come. She put a plate of cupcakes in front of me then mentioned she'd seen you through the window. Please come over for a little while. Neighbors need each other at times like this."

How could Wesley say no? He couldn't.

∽℔

SATURDAY, *10 a.m. No change.*

Kass printed the words onto the white board above the display case then initialed them. The board normally offered the day's specials, but the special on the day after Al Santoro's accident was prayer, and the board was updated with every text or call someone received from a family member. A basket sat beside it, rapidly filling with envelopes — cards and well-wishes from neighbors and friends that someone would take up to the hospital later.

Lenore tied an apron around her waist. "Where's Celeste?"

Kass grimaced. "She didn't show up. I phoned, and the call went to voice mail. A few minutes later she texted to say she was sorry she couldn't make it in today."

"Fired?" Lenore raised her eyebrows.

"If only we had someone to replace her. I'm not sure if today will be super busy or super quiet as everyone is focused on Al's family."

"That woman the other day left an application form."

Astrid Jansen. The problem was, Kass did not want to hire Wesley's ex-mother-in-law, even though the position was entry level and didn't actually require any prior experience. Her relationship to Wesley aside, the woman was anti-sugar. How could she possibly be a good fit for a bakery?

Just then Jasmine pulled open the door and stumbled in, eyes bloodshot, long hair pulled into a lopsided ponytail. The entire area went quiet in an instant.

Kass froze beside the counter, staring at her friend.

"The other driver was under the influence," Jasmine spat out. "Point one two blood alcohol level. Her airbag went off, and she walked away."

Hailey stepped beside Kass, swaying.

Kass put an arm around her cousin. "In the middle of a Friday afternoon." She could ask how that could be, but facts were facts, and alcoholics didn't necessarily follow a timetable.

"Can you believe it?" Jasmine growled. "Makes me doubly glad my stupid brother is in jail. At least it wasn't him behind the wheel. At least he was pulled over before someone got hurt."

"Basil will take this badly." Hailey put a hand on the counter to steady herself.

Jasmine gave Hailey a hard look. "And so he should."

"Does he know what's going on?"

"Dad just went over to the jail to tell him. Dad is so

much nicer than I am. I'd probably punch Basil's lights out all over again."

"But he didn't hit Al's truck," murmured Hailey.

Jasmine leaned in, eyes flashing. "He's lucky. That's all I can say. When I think how blind we all were to the magnitude of Basil's drinking problem, I want to explode. This could've been him."

Basil was midway through a thirty-day jail sentence for his June DUI conviction. Kass prayed this would be a wakeup call for the Santoro black sheep.

"Have they released the other driver's name?" someone called out.

"Yes." Jasmine grabbed the dry erase marker and wrote under Kass's recent notation. "She's a neighbor of the Rantas out on West Riverside. She ran that stop sign down from the school — going at least eighty — and rammed straight into Uncle Al's door as his truck went through the intersection."

A small sob escaped Hailey, and she covered her face with her hands.

The door to the street opened, and Wesley stepped through, his son at his side.

Kass desperately wanted to fly across the intervening space and find safety and comfort in his arms, but how could she? Not after the way they'd left each other last week. Not knowing he wasn't a believer.

What if it had been him hit by the drunk driver? What if, instead of hanging on as Al was doing, Wesley had been ushered into God's presence? Like Sydney had. How many chances did a person get?

Wesley's gaze locked on hers.

She could see the anguish in his eyes from here. How could Al's accident hit him so hard? He probably hadn't spoken five words with the older man, unless he'd gotten a quote for a tree trimming. Kass couldn't remember any more than that Wesley's yard was fully treed. She hadn't been looking at them, only at the handsome man who'd gazed deeply into her eyes.

She couldn't get those kisses out of her mind. She didn't really want to, because they might be all the romance she had in her life forever. Good men interested in a busy entrepreneur didn't pop up just everywhere. Who knew Hailey's and her success would scare men away?

It hadn't scared Wesley. Nothing had, other than her preaching the gospel to his face after he'd kissed her. And she'd done a lousy job of presenting truth, her words all jumbled and messed up, warring with her desire to ignore the warnings in her mind.

She hadn't seen him since, except in church. Which rang of irony, come to think of it.

Are you okay? he mouthed.

On one side of her, Hailey sniffled quietly. On the other, Jasmine railed against the drunk driver with nearby sympathetic patrons.

Was she okay? Not really. She shook her head slightly.

Wesley turned one hand toward her — not a grand gesture. Not something likely to catch the attention of anyone else.

Kass took two steps toward him then hesitated.

His hand stayed steady. So did his gaze.

She needed steady. She crossed the space but brushed past him out onto the bistro's patio. The door clicked shut behind her, and she turned. He was right there, and she melted into his arms, pulling Sebastian in as well. The little guy clung to her waist. It was too late to shield her heart or Sebastian's. Wesley's, too, by the tightness of his arms around her.

What was she going to do about it? Could they remain friends and not more? She didn't see how, not when everything in her craved his touch.

But Lenore had traveled this path, falling in love with someone weak in faith. Lenore, who'd left Dad because he'd taken her for granted. But couldn't a marriage where both were solid believers still suffer from inattention? Sure, they could. Marriage was work. Kass knew that, if only from observation.

And yet, without Lenore, where would Kass be now? Her stepmother had made all the difference for the child and teen Kass had been. Without Lenore, she wouldn't have stayed in church, gone to summer camp and youth group, or trusted Jesus as her personal Savior the summer she was twelve.

A loving, faithful stepmother could work miracles. It might be different when the child in question was male, though Sebastian's face buried against her hip spoke of his need.

"Are you close to the family?" Wesley murmured softly.

"Everyone is," she replied with shaky breath. "The Santoros have lived right here in Bridgeview for probably a hundred years. Jasmine's great-grandparents built a house where the community garden stands now."

He shook his head. "I can't imagine that kind of continuity."

"Me, either. My family sure doesn't have it. Is yours close?"

He scoffed lightly. "No."

"I'm not sure if a large close family is a blessing or not, when I see how all the Santoros are hurting right now. Al and Winnie's son Dominic got in from Seattle around midnight last night. Al's brother Matt came from Galena Landing. One nephew came from Helena and another from Twin Falls. Everyone is just at Deaconess, together, waiting."

"It's worse to have no one. Trust me."

Kass looked up at him. "No one?"

His eyes were hard and flat. "No one who cares."

"I can't imagine. I've always had my dad. My grandparents, until about five years ago. My cousin. There aren't many of us, but we care for each other."

"I was raised in foster care."

She caught her breath. "I'm so sorry."

"It wasn't a picnic." He stared at her as though

daring her to refute him. "I meant it when I said no one cared."

Kass had heard about dozens of loving foster families, but it made sense some were in it only for the money. She longed to wipe away the negative memories that lingered in the depths of Wesley's eyes, wished she could comfort the young boy he'd been. "I don't know how I would have managed without knowing the love of God as the biggest constant in my life. He promises to be the Father to those who don't have one. He sets the lonely in families."

"He never gave me one. Not for long, anyway."

The little boy pressing against them shifted restlessly.

"But you have Sebastian now. You're a family together."

"Yeah." His voice choked. "Yeah, we are."

She had to ask. "Do you know Al well?"

"I don't think I've ever met the guy."

Kass tilted her head back. "Then why...?"

"It's hard not to notice how it affects everyone. The sense of community here is unlike anything I've ever known. I've always felt on the outside looking in, but this place is threatening to suck me all the way in. These people. What is it, Kass?"

"I think it's Jesus," she said softly. "The Santoros have always been pillars of the church as well as of the community, but it's more than them. So many of our neighbors — not all of them, of course — have found a foundational belonging in the family of God. Scripture says, 'Though my father and mother forsake me, the Lord will receive me.' My mom left me by dying." Wesley hadn't told her what happened to his parents. She wouldn't push him. "My dad became distant, lost in his own grief, until he met Lenore. She made us into a family again... but it wasn't really her. It was God working through her."

"I told Myles it seems crazy. This whole God thing."

Her heart sped up that he'd been talking to Myles about the Lord. "I can see why it might seem that way."

"So, is God going to answer everyone's prayers for this man?"

"Time will tell." But the longer Al Santoro remained on life support without awakening, the lower his chances were. The doctors had set his broken bones, removed his spleen, and cauterized the internal bleeding, hoping for a positive change by morning. A change that hadn't come. Not yet.

"Will people still trust Him if He doesn't?"

Kass met Wesley's eyes. "Yes."

He raised his brows.

"Okay, there are no guarantees that each person's faith will remain intact if the worst happens. We're individuals, and there isn't a universal response. If you're asking if people automatically trust God all the time after they become Christians, then no, of course not. But God dwells within us through His Holy Spirit, and we have the capacity to hold on, growing closer to Him through the hard times."

"I don't like hard times. I've had too many of my own."

"I get it." She really did. But could the tiny bit of faith that was trying to sprout in Wesley Ferguson withstand this big storm? She'd pray it would take root and grow. For the sake of his eternal soul.

CHAPTER 18

*W*esley looked around the Spokane mega-church, his fingers tightening around Sebastian's. The sheer number of people gathered for Al Santoro's celebration of life — wasn't that a weird thing to call a funeral? — was overwhelming. All of Bridgeview had shut down, the elementary school included, since everyone knew and apparently loved the youngest of the Santoro brothers. Half the remaining population of Spokane seemed to know the man as well, as the vast auditorium was packed on both levels. The arborist must've impacted many people's lives.

How many people would come to Wesley's funeral should he die? Sebastian would be flanked by Astrid and Robert. Kass might come, but how much would she mourn? Myles and Adriana... a few others who would rattle in Bridgeview Bible Church, which didn't have anywhere near the capacity to hold the crowd here for Al Santoro.

Wesley's life impacted no one but his son's. What was the key? Just being born into a large family, marrying a lovely woman like Winnie — whom Wesley had only met babysitting at the cooking club — and having five kids of his own? More than that. The whole community loved this man. Tissues dabbed eyes everywhere.

The family filed in. Winnie and Marietta with Winnie and Al's children. Ray and Grace's family, including Kass's friend Jasmine, her fiancé, and Marco's family. Dino and Betta's family, with their son, Peter, and two young women, one on crutches and the other cradling a baby. Franco and Genevera, whom Wesley didn't know as well, with two young families. Another group, the man clearly a Santoro by his dark good looks, with a woman and two adult kids.

The organ swelled with music as Logan Dermott, back from Edmonds for the funeral, asked everyone to rise. Lyrics popped up on multiple screens.

"When peace, like a river, attendeth my way, when sorrows like sea billows roll; whatever my lot, Thou hast taught me to say, 'it is well, it is well with my soul.'"

Down in the front center pew, the widow stood with an arm around each of her youngest two sons, Michael and a teen. She stared toward the screen, and her lips moved with the music.

Really? Wesley looked from Winnie to the lyrics then back again. He could understand the words about sorrows like sea billows. Those made sense, especially in context. He remembered that pain even at Sydney's death, and they'd barely been on speaking terms. But peace? Still believing one's soul was in good hands?

That was more than he could comprehend, but it matched up to what he'd been reading in John. He'd read that one paragraph so many times the words were stuck in his brain. Jesus said, "Everyone who drinks this water will be thirsty again, but whoever drinks the water I give them will never thirst. Indeed, the water I give them will become in them a spring of water welling up to eternal life."

Because Wesley had lingered so long on that section of the fourth chapter, words from the seventh had thrummed when he read them last night. Jesus had said, "Let anyone who is thirsty come to me and drink. Whoever believes in me, as Scripture has said, living water will flow from within them."

It looked like everyone in this auditorium had sipped that living water, or maybe gulped it. Dove in it and swam.

Wesley read the rest of the words to the song. *He lives — oh the bliss of this glorious thought; my sin, not in part, but the whole is nailed to His cross, and I bear it no more. Praise the Lord, praise the Lord, oh my soul.*

Pastor Tomas had spoken of forgiven sin that Sunday a couple of weeks back. Now he delivered another sermon on the topic, and Wesley drank in the words of living water.

Beside him, a tall man about his own age scrunched a baseball cap between his hands, his hair tousled as though it hadn't been brushed before the cap landed on it this morning. He wasn't in his Sunday best like everyone else but wore tattered, grass-stained jeans and a T-shirt. Yet the guy leaned forward, elbows on his knees, and riveted his attention on Pastor Tomas.

As the service came to a close, the man blinked a few times before turning to Wesley. "Have you ever heard that before?"

"Just in the past few weeks. I moved into Bridgeview recently, and I've been going to Pastor Tomas's church."

"I should do that. My sister and brother-in-law keep talking about Jesus as though He's real and someone I should meet. But today... today it kind of makes sense. Al was a good man. A really good man."

"You knew him?" Did Wesley dare admit that he didn't?

"Worked with him many a time. I'm a landscaper. If one of my clients' trees needed a good trim, I'd always recommend Al Santoro. He talked to me about Jesus, too." He twisted the baseball cap in his hands and chuckled. "He talked to *everybody* about Jesus. And yet everyone liked him."

"Myles Sheridan's been telling me."

The man nodded. "Another good one." He stuck out his hand. "Dan Ranta, by the way."

"Wesley Ferguson and my son, Sebastian. I bought the old Davenport place along the river."

"I know the property. Good to see it's not vacant anymore. I'm looking for a rental in the area for me and my girlfriend and our three kids. Hear of anything?"

Wesley shook his head. "Not off-hand, no. It's a tight market." He followed the other man into the fellowship hall where a vast array of sandwiches and squares adorned long tables. Apparently the deceased had been laid to rest earlier this morning, with only family at the graveside. Strange way to run a funeral, but whatever. It meant no processional... and that everyone was present in the room now.

Hailey carried a platter of sandwiches out to a table, while Kass removed an empty coffee urn. No wonder he hadn't caught sight of her in the multitude. She'd been busy with preparation on top of sharing the community's grief.

He made his way toward her, drawn like a fish on a line, as she stood surveying the tables. "Kass?"

Her sweet smile tipped the world right-side-up again. "Hi, Wesley." She bent to pull Sebastian to her side for a brief moment. "Hey, little bean."

And his boy hugged her back, as though it were the most natural thing in the world... while Astrid stared with narrowed eyes from near the kitchen doors.

"WHAT'S ASTRID DOING HERE?"

Kass tried not to grimace. "We needed help, desperately, and she'd put in an application. She came in yesterday and spent all day making sandwiches."

"You needed a lot of them." Wesley gestured to the tables, where family and friends of the Santoros made their way down both sides, helping themselves to a luncheon in Al's honor. "It didn't occur to me they'd ask you to cater."

"We were the family's first choice. In Bridgeview, you do whatever you can for each other, whether it's helping a grieving family, or hiring a neighborhood business when you have an event. Even a sad one."

Astrid slung an arm over Sebastian's shoulder. "Hello, little man. I didn't expect to see you here."

"Hi, Gigi. N-No school today."

The last thing Kass wanted was for Astrid to clue into the sparks between Wesley and her. She took a step back. "There's a plate I need to replace."

"Want me to get it?"

"Sure. In the middle of the fourth table." Kass hadn't meant to send Astrid, but why not? The result was the same, hopefully keeping Sebastian's grandmother from noticing the way Kass couldn't keep her eyes off Wesley.

Astrid scurried away, and Kass did her best to keep her exhale silent, especially with Wesley so near her senses were filled with the fragrance of his woodsy cologne.

"That was quite the sermon." Wesley's eye locked onto hers. "Did you hear it?"

She nodded. "We sat right by the doors so we could slip out before the closing prayer and uncover the sandwiches." She hesitated. "What part are you talking about?"

He laughed shortly. "All of it. Starting with that *It is Well with My Soul* song and ending with the *come to Jesus* bit."

Kass's body tensed, and the air in the fellowship hall sizzled around the three of them, blocking all other sounds, smells, and visuals. She'd withdrawn as Pastor Tomas had leaned over the podium and asked if there was anyone present who needed to give their life to Jesus today. Had Wesley responded? Did she dare ask?

"It's starting to make sense to me."

Her heart danced with joy. She smiled at him. "From there it's just a step of faith. Of deciding to go forward and praying the rest will reveal itself as you get there."

"Like the Romans Road."

She blinked, the visual of the twisting road on the screen glimmering in her memory. "Yes. We can't see around the curves or into the distance. All we need to see is the next step."

"Kass?" Shay looked between them. "Sorry to

bother you, but we're out of tuna sandwiches as well as chicken salad. What do you want me to do?"

Well, certainly not make more. Kass scanned the tables and the crowd in the large room. "Looks like nearly everyone is through the line. I think it will be fine. Can you and Lenore consolidate the remains to one table? And make sure all the coffee carafes are full."

"You've got it." Shay scurried away.

"I should let you go." Wesley's hand was warm on her arm. "But... can we talk? Later?"

After this event she'd be so exhausted she'd want to sleep for a week. Not that she had the luxury. But the thought of the quiet darkness along the river behind Wesley's house was a close second. Add in his arms, the thought of his kisses, and the words of burgeoning faith he'd just spoken? There was definitely nowhere she'd rather be this evening.

"It'll probably be after eight before I'm free."

A hint of a grin played across his face. "Sounds perfect. Sebastian is in bed by seven."

"I'll see you then." His fingers caressed her arm for a few seconds before dropping to his side.

Kass turned away before she took his arm and waltzed out of the fellowship hall with him right then and there. She nearly rammed straight into Dan Ranta. "Excuse me, please."

But Dan was focused beyond her. "I'm sorry. Your brother was a good man."

Ray Santoro stood facing Dan. "He was the best." Sorrow choked the man's voice.

Kass edged out from between them.

"He told me some of the same stuff the pastor said today. Is that really all it is? Just believing? Logan's talked about it, too."

"It's that simple. Not easy, but simple."

Dan sounded like Wesley. How many people might have heard the message of Jesus' gift of eternal life today who had never really considered it before? Kass breathed a prayer for Dan even as she realized his girlfriend wasn't with him. Had anyone shared Jesus with Dixie? Dan's sister, Linnea, had, but did Dixie have any Christian friends now that Linnea and Logan had moved away?

Kass rarely saw Dixie. The family didn't live in the neighborhood, and Dixie didn't frequent the bistro. If God was calling Kass to be the other woman's friend, how would she even get to know her? Guess that would be God's problem.

Dan shook his head. "I'm looking for a rental in Bridgeview. Do you know of any?"

Kass grinned as she lingered, totally eavesdropping. Dan asked that question of everyone he met.

"My mother's rental is empty."

Dan scoffed. "She won't rent to me since Dixie and I aren't married." He lowered his voice. "I'd marry her if she'd only say yes. I want my son to have a stable home. I'd even adopt her other kids."

Kass held her breath at the plaintive longing in Dan's voice.

"I'll talk to Mamma. I can't guarantee anything, you understand. She's been praying for the right renter while turning everyone away as they come to the door."

"Thanks, Ray. All I ask is a chance."

"No problem, Dan. Do you want to talk about Pastor Tomas's message now? I'd be happy to answer any questions you might have."

Oh, right. Kass should be waiting tables and cleaning the kitchen, not glued to a conversation that wasn't her own. She shifted away, glancing over her shoulder a few seconds later to see Ray and Dan taking seats at a table on the side wall, out of the melee.

Lord, please give Ray words. Thank You that he's willing and able to see someone else's need even while he grieves for his brother.

CHAPTER 19

The cousins and their staff unloaded the borrowed truck at the back of the bistro. Kass carried a load of tablecloths in and caught sight of the flashing light on the business answering machine. After starting the washing machine, she poked the button to hear the message.

"Sorry I couldn't make it today." Celeste's voice.

Today? How about all the other days? Kass raised her eyebrows and kept listening as Hailey and Astrid stopped beside her, Lenore and Shay right behind them.

"I might be a little late in the morning, but I'll be there!"

"Well, isn't she Miss Sunshine," Lenore said drily.

Shay rolled her eyes. "Fi-erd," she announced.

Kass met Hailey's gaze. "I don't think we have a choice." But Lenore was only temporary, and Astrid had been hired only for the event. Kass wouldn't have called Wesley's ex's mom if she'd had any other choice. Sure there'd been a few other applications from students and those who specified which hours they were available — ones which didn't match the hours they were needed.

"If you're shorthanded tomorrow, maybe I could come in. Sounds like you need me."

Of course Astrid would offer.

Hailey lifted her shoulder just barely and dropped it. Code for Kass getting to decide. "Sure. If you can be here by seven, we'll give it a try for the rest of the week and see how it goes."

"You won't be sorry."

Oh, yes, she would.

"Let's get the rest of the truck unloaded," suggested Hailey. "Astrid, would you mind repackaging what we can take over to Winnie's house? With all that out-of-town company, I'm sure she can put it to good use."

Lenore remained beside Kass in the back hall. "I think God sent us Astrid for a reason," she said quietly.

"You *know* why she's a bad idea."

"Is it the sugar thing... or Wesley?" Lenore pulled her into the office and shut the door. "Sweetie, I'm concerned about you. I don't want to see you making the same mistake I did."

Kass stared at her stepmother, her heart sinking. "I needed you. How was that a mistake?"

"Oh, honey. That's not what I meant."

She was way, way too tired for this. Everyone had tiptoed around Bridgeview for over a week while Al's life hung in the balance. The atmosphere hadn't changed much in the days up until the funeral. All she wanted was a long kiss in the moonlight and then a solid night's sleep. Not a heart-to-heart with a stepmother in confession mode. She crossed her arms and raised her chin. "What do you mean, then?"

"Those are two separate issues. I'm so glad God gave me the honor of being your mom."

Kass raised her eyebrows.

"But I knew your dad was weak in faith. I foolishly thought he'd be drawn closer to the Lord through me, but it didn't happen that way."

"You couldn't have it both ways."

"Be your mom without being Farrell's wife? You're right. I couldn't."

"I'm not sure what you're saying here. The situation is very different. You didn't hear Wesley today. He's an active seeker."

"And he has a child who desperately needs a mother figure, like a little girl I once knew."

"Again, it's different."

Lenore shook her head. "It's always different. No two people or situations are alike. I only see too many similarities for me to keep my mouth shut. I don't want to see you hurt."

"But things are different for Dad now. He's been coming to counseling with you every week."

"I've got your dad over a barrel with that. He wants me to come back, and I promised I would when Ava comes back to work next week... so long as he doesn't miss a session. And he hasn't."

"He knows you'll come back regardless." Kass let out a shaky breath. "Wouldn't you?"

Lenore sighed. "I would. I love him, and I love you. I don't want to break the family apart. I couldn't keep living the way it was forever, but I honestly don't know if the counseling is doing as much good as I'd hoped. He's going through the motions."

Too much information. Kass didn't doubt that her father loved his wife. But, yes, he took her for granted. He always had. He'd been desperate for someone to take care of his daughter and the house, and Lenore had stepped right into the gap.

Was that the same as Wesley? One big difference was that Kass couldn't be Suzy Homemaker like Lenore had become over twenty years ago. The business took far too much of her time. But did she only want to make Wesley and his son's life easier? More complete? No. She loved him.

Whoa. Really?

She stared at Lenore, unwilling to even think the thought in her stepmother's presence. "Thank you for sharing your heart, but we need to get back and give the others a hand."

Lenore nodded. "You're right."

HEADLIGHTS SPUN an arc in the falling darkness as a vehicle turned into Wesley's drive, crunching gravel. Then the engine of Kass's Rav4 cut out. Her car door shut on the other side of the house.

He waited in the shadowed backyard, too restless to sit in one of the two deck chairs he'd set on the freshly-mowed grass.

"Wesley?" Her voice was low as she rounded the back of the house.

His heart stuttered. "I'm here." And then he couldn't wait any longer, but crossed the space. Her gentle fragrance flooded him as he slid his arms around her waist and drew her close.

Kass looped her hands behind his neck and touched her forehead to his.

He liked that she nearly matched him in height. Liked the swish of her long locks brushing his fore-arms, liked the fit of her light sweater skimming her form beneath his hands. Liked the way her lips reached for his as eagerly as his did for hers.

A few weeks ago, she'd walked away from him, saying it could never work. What had spurred the change, he wasn't completely certain, but he wasn't about to complain. Not when the woman of his dreams molded her body, her lips, against his.

"Kass," he groaned between desperate mint-flavored kisses.

She pulled away first. He'd expected her to, with the principles she'd cited last time they'd kissed right here by the river, though he'd been careful not to cross any lines. She was too important for that. Whatever she needed — whatever crumbs she'd give him — would be enough. Almost enough.

"Oh, Wesley. It's been so crazy." She sighed, resting her head against his.

"I know," he murmured.

"We talked about forever, remember?"

Oh, he remembered, all right. The thoughts of this woman forever in his arms had taunted him since. He nodded and kissed her ear.

"What does that even mean?" she whispered.

He pulled back, angling her to see into her eyes from the porch light next door. "The word keeps cropping up."

"Winnie thought she'd have a lifetime with Al."

Wesley had thought he'd have a lifetime with Sydney, but she'd left him in every possible way.

"I thought my dad and stepmom were solid, but I didn't see the cracks in their marriage."

Where was she going with this? Unease began to flutter at the edges of his vision.

"Lenore says she's going back to Idaho next week when Ava's cleared to return to work, but she doesn't think their separation has made the big changes she'd hoped and prayed for." Kass looked in his eyes and sucked in her lower lip.

Wesley kissed her, teasing at her lip until she responded, but then she pushed away again. "How do you know when it's going to last forever?"

Was she asking about their relationship, or was the question broader? He doubted she realized how it bounced inside his head and sounded to him. Could he do forever with this woman? He'd known her less than two months, but he couldn't envision doing life without her... or with anyone but her. She was it. He was sunk.

He chose his words carefully. "You said a couple has to be going the same direction, but that wasn't enough for Al and Winnie."

"Life is so cruel. When I think of Winnie, those kids, especially those younger boys who need their dad so much, it just chokes me right up. They *need* Al, Wesley. They need him."

"Aren't you the one who told me God is in control? And Pastor Tomas talked about that at the funeral, too."

A sob rent her throat, and she clutched him close. Not that he was complaining as he rubbed her back with long, soothing strokes.

"I know, right? I've been a believer nearly all my life, and I'm having such a hard time with this. I don't know why I'm dumping it all on you, when you don't even know if you believe in God."

"Who said?"

She sniffled. "You did. Lenore was right. I shouldn't be here."

Lenore? What did she have to do with anything? Kass's dad's marriage shouldn't be part of this conversation. Her stepmom shouldn't be interfering. Kass was twenty-eight, not eighteen. "Don't write me off so quickly, sweetheart," he murmured into her neck. "I told you I've been thinking, and I mean a *lot*. About everything Pastor Tomas has said in his sermons and at the funeral today, about things Myles has said, and even Marco when we took the boys to the playground one day before his uncle's accident. It's a lot to process, Kass, so different from anything I knew as a child. I'm working through it as quickly as I can."

"But you can't do it for me."

"You keep saying that, but I don't know what you mean."

"I mean... I think that's what my dad did. He wanted Lenore so much — I'm not saying you want me—"

"But I do." Wesley kissed her again.

She pulled back. "He wanted her so much he went to church and learned the lingo to make her happy. I'm not saying he totally pretended, but his faith isn't strong on his own. He let me go to Sunday School with the neighbors, but when he met Lenore, he started coming to church, too. H-he fooled her into thinking he wanted a genuine relationship with God."

"And you're worried I'm doing the same thing?"

"Well, yes. I can't help but notice the similarities. I remember the desperately needy little kid I was, wanting a mom so much. Lenore was everything I'd been longing for."

"So their marriage was a good thing."

"For me. I'm not sure if it was for her. And I look at Sebastian, and I see myself all over aga—" She clapped her hand over her mouth and whirled out of his arms.

"Sweetheart..."

"No. I said too much."

"You're envisioning marrying me, being my wife and Sebastian's mother. It's no more than I've dreamed myself, sweetheart. I can't help but really, really like the concept."

"But..."

"I'm not your father, Kass. I'm not saying I'm better than him or worse than him. All I know is I'm different from him. You're not Lenore. Sebastian isn't you as a child. Don't you think we need to see where our own story leads? It's exclusively ours, a unique blend of flavors. Just like we are."

Kass stood a few feet away, arms wrapped around her middle, staring at him. "Wesley? I'm afraid. I'm afraid I've... fallen for you. I'm not good at this waiting thing."

"You're not alone. I'm head over heels for you. I can't imagine the emptiness without you in my life. But I know you're right. I have to find the answers to my questions. In fact, Sebastian and I are going to the Ramirezes' house for dinner tomorrow, and Pastor Tomas and I will start that conversation. This isn't for fear of losing what you and I have. Not really. It's because I've seen something in you. Something in Myles and Adriana and Tomas and Juanita and Marco and Daria and... nearly everyone I've met in Bridgeview. I've faced that I'm empty and broken inside — have been all my life — and I'm *this* close to finding the answers. I can feel it. I can taste it, it's so close. Please, Kass, can you be patient with me just a little longer?"

She moved a bit closer as the moon began to lift above the house, setting her glorious hair aglow. "You're not just saying that?"

"I'm not. I wouldn't lie to you. You're too important for that, and so is this subject."

"I'll give you time," she whispered. "All the time you need." And she closed the gap, tangled her fingers with his, and kissed him.

CHAPTER 20

The doorbell rang late Friday evening. It had been a long, busy day, and Kass was exhausted. Shifting Ava back into the schedule wasn't as easy as she'd hoped. Between Ava's grief at her uncle's death and the fact that her leg was weak after so long in a cast, the transition was going to take a bit of time. It didn't help that Lenore was gone and she'd had to fire Celeste. They were still short-staffed. Still needed Astrid.

"I've got it," hollered Hailey.

Kass tucked her feet up under herself on the sofa. Hopefully it would be for Hailey. Something quick. Kass craved quiet evenings to recharge.

Until she heard a male voice, and her heart kicked up a beat. Wesley? It couldn't be. He was home this time of day, with Sebastian in bed. But if it wasn't him, had Hailey attracted a man at long last? Kass couldn't think whom it might be, so she unpretzeled herself and wandered the few steps through to the kitchen.

Wesley. He looked past Hailey's shoulder, and his blue eyes warmed as a tiny smile hitched the corner of his mouth into his short beard. There was something different about him, not just that his sidekick was missing.

"Kassidy. I brought something for you." He glanced at her cousin. "For both of you, really." He lifted a brown paper bag with twine handles toward her.

Hailey stepped closer, her eyes gleaming with curiosity.

Kass searched Wesley's face. "What is it?" Because this was odd. A gift for her, maybe, although this would be the first time. But something for her and Hailey both?

He grinned. "Open it and see."

The bag was heavier than she expected, and filled with crumpled newsprint. She set the bag on the kitchen island, reached inside, and wrapped her fingers around the thin edge of a plate — a plate? She sent him a questioning gaze as she withdrew the object.

Hailey's gasp made Kass look down. Grandma's gorgeous Tuscan Works plate with gilded handles sat in her hands, in one piece again. Whole, but wholly different, now seamed with gold.

"What is that?" Hailey's voice choked off.

Long past time for full disclosure. Kass swallowed hard. "Remember the anniversary celebration back in

August? I made a snap decision to bring this scalloped plate down and put lemon squares on it."

Hailey's arms crossed. "Uh huh."

"It got broken. I'm so sorry."

Her cousin's eyebrows shot into her hair even as her chin dipped. "You put a priceless heirloom down where people could grab things off it and bump into it and—"

"It was Sebastian." Wesley's voice broke in.

Kass couldn't let the child take the blame. "But it was my fault."

"You bet your sweet bootie it's your fault. I wondered where that plate went. It used to be up on the high shelf that now seems to be full of birds made of nuts and bolts." Hailey sent Wesley a glare.

"I can remove those—"

"The birds are selling, Wesley." Kass blinked back tears, trying to clear her eyes and focus on the plate. A gold line, matching the outlines around the tiny white flowers, crossed the white center, intersecting with other seams spider-webbing through the duck-egg-blue border. "And this is beautiful. Look at it, Hailey. I know I blew it. Even worse, I didn't own up to it. I'm so sorry but, please. Just look." She nudged the plate closer to her cousin.

Hailey turned it around on the counter before looking up at Wesley. "How did you do this?"

He looked between them then traced a gold seam with one fingertip. "It's an ancient Japanese art called kintsugi. We often throw away things that are broken, or else we try to patch them up, but the value is gone. The beauty is shattered."

Hailey studied him, gnawing on her lower lip.

Kass closed her eyes. He was talking about more than old plates.

"Instead of treating broken things with dishonor, Japanese artists began infusing them with honor by mending them with gold. Instead of trying to hide the fractures like most of us would do, they celebrated every crack by highlighting it with gold, showcasing the beauty in something that is flawed. Imperfect."

"Grandma would have loved this," Hailey said softly.

Kass stared at her cousin. Had she heard correctly?

But Hailey's anger had dissipated completely as her pink-tipped finger traced a gold seam. "She was all about seeing the best in people. Remember that?"

Kass nodded. "She hated throwing away broken things."

"She hated throwing away anything." Hailey laughed. "We had a lot of sorting to do when we inherited the building."

Kass remembered. So many objects, many with memories attached... more so for Hailey, who'd lived with their grandparents, than for her. Sure, some had been obvious junk. Grandma had seemed unable to recycle even a plastic bag.

"I kept that broken teapot." Hailey glanced at Kass.

"I couldn't bear to toss it, when Grandma poured tea from it for little girls so often."

"The one with pink roses."

Her cousin nodded then looked at Wesley. "Do you think you could...?"

"I'll have a look."

Kass stepped toward him as Hailey disappeared into her room. "I know I should have told her what happened. There never seemed to be a good time, but that's a lousy excuse."

He held out his hands. "You're human. Who wants to admit mistakes?"

She twined her fingers with his. He looked so good. Smelled so good. "I've been talking to you about Jesus, but I didn't show you by my life."

"You did." He brushed his lips over hers, running an electric tingle through her body. "You've showed me so much. What's more, my life is a lot like this plate."

She pulled back just enough that she could see deeply into his eyes. "How's that?"

"Broken in so many ways. A messed-up childhood where no one wanted me."

The thought crushed her. At least she'd had her dad. He'd tried.

"A desperate search for love, which only led to more cracks. Splinters. Fractures." He glanced down at the plate beside them then focused on her eyes again. "Everything was broken, Kass. Into a million jillion pieces, like Sebastian would say."

She managed a crooked smile.

"But you... you helped the edges align again."

"No—"

His finger touched her mouth, stopping her words. "You couldn't fix me. You knew that. But you helped. And then Jesus came along and performed kintsugi on me. He took all my broken pieces and melded them together. I guess in Christian lingo He did it with blood, not gold — still sounds mighty weird to me — but it's kind of the same thing."

Her heart soared. "You got all that from the Gospel of John?"

Wesley shook his head. "Not all. I've spent hours this week with Pastor Tomas. He's a very patient man, answering every question as many ways as it took to get the concepts through my thick skull. I've spent so much time there in the past couple of days that our sons are now best friends, and Sebastian is having a sleepover with Isaac tonight."

That answered the question Kass had nearly forgotten about — his son's whereabouts — but it was minor compared to everything else he'd said. "I'm so happy for you." For herself, too. Her heart felt like a door had opened to the most appetizing picnic, spreading to the horizon and beyond. Birds sang, butterflies danced in the air, and mottled sunlight shone on long tables spread with white cloths, loaded with a tantalizing smorgasbord of flavors and aromas.

The possibilities were endless.

WESLEY CRADLED Kass's face with both hands as her hands settled on his hips. Her brown eyes seemed lit from within, and her pink lips parted as he leaned closer, taking his time, drinking in the sight of her, the fragrance of her.

"It's possible I'm interrupting something," Hailey said drily.

The schoolboy in him demanded he drop his hands, but the man in him smiled ruefully into the eyes of his beloved instead. He pressed another quick kiss to Kass's lips. "Nothing that can't wait." Which cousin he spoke to, he wasn't sure.

Kass smiled back, gently, then turned toward her cousin as Hailey set an ice cream bucket on the island and popped off the lid.

He wrapped an arm around Kass and leaned toward the container, every atom of his being aware of her proximity, heightened when her hand slipped around his back and her thumb hooked through the belt loop of his jeans.

A jagged crack lined the teapot's body right through the delicately hand-painted roses, and the spout had broken off. No wonder Hailey had kept it. It must have seemed like a sprinkle of golden fairy dust would be all that was required to repair the antique. He had that dust aplenty.

Wesley ran his finger gently down the crack. "That's

a beautiful piece. I'll have to break it all the way through, but I think a light tap will do it."

"If it breaks into a couple of extra pieces, it won't make much difference, will it?" Hailey's eyes pleaded with his.

"None at all." He glanced at her. "So long as you know it can't be used for tea. The epoxy and gold dust aren't food-safe."

"It can go up on the shelf beside this plate."

"If we move Wesley's birds off it."

"Well, yes..."

He chuckled. "It's also not difficult to add a shelf or two. Or I can hang my pieces directly on the plank walls. There are options."

"There are always options."

Kass's words seemed to be layered with meaning, but she was right. Pastor Tomas had cautioned Wesley, though, about moving too quickly with Kass. He seemed to think Wesley needed time to mature as a new believer before moving forward. The man was probably right, much as Wesley hated to admit it.

"We can talk about that another time." Hailey looked between them. "I'm just, um, going to get a ginger ale and go read in my room. Maybe turn in early tonight." She strolled to the fridge, placing her hand over her yawning mouth.

For real? Wesley glanced at Kass, who laughed outright. "Thanks, Hailey."

Her cousin plucked a can from the shelf and turned

toward them, eyebrows raised over twinkling eyes. "You owe me one."

"I'll keep it in mind."

"See that you do." Hailey popped the tab and saluted with the can. "Good night." Then she disappeared down the short hallway.

Wesley turned to Kass. "Now, where were we?"

CHAPTER 21

I could have found someone else. Are you sure you're okay?" Kass angled a look at Winnie in the community center kitchen. It had only been two weeks since Al's funeral. Shouldn't his wife still be mourning instead of watching other people's kids for cooking club?

"I need as much normal as possible." Winnie tucked shoulder-length brown hair behind her ear. "The kids have gone back to school, and I can't keep staring at my four walls every day."

"No, I get that." Kass gave the older woman a side hug. "No one expects anything of you, though. Take all the time you need."

"How many little ones will be here today?"

"Four or five. There's Rebekah now with Olivia."

Winnie stretched her arms out and the one-year-old reached back.

"Thanks, Winnie." Rebekah relinquished the toddler. "Are you sure?"

"Of course, I'm sure. I need to keep busy." The widow nuzzled Olivia's neck. The little one giggled, bringing a smile that touched Winnie's eyes.

"If you need to talk, my door is always open."

That was the psych major in Rebekah speaking, as though she didn't have enough on her plate. Wasn't she back counseling at Bridgeview Elementary halftime now that Olivia was in Fran's daycare?

"I appreciate your offer, thanks. I'll keep it in mind."

Was that code for *no, thank you*? It often was when Kass said it.

Rebekah turned to Kass. "So what's this I hear about you and Bridgeview's newest resident?"

"Me and Dan Ranta? He's oh, so taken." Kass smirked.

Dan and Dixie had spent last weekend moving into Marietta's rental with their three kids. Well, Dixie's three kids. Only the youngest was Dan's.

"Funny girl. You know whom I mean."

Winnie's eyes brightened. "Fill me in."

"Have you met the guy who moved into the old Davenport place next door to Adriana's? Single dad with a little guy in first grade." Rebekah waggled her brows at Kass. "You may have noticed him at church. Not only that, but he's been seen wandering the riverbank with our own Kassidy North."

She should have known the permaculture forest between Rebekah and Wade's house and the riverfront pathway wasn't thick enough to block the view from the Ropers' dining room window. Kass could feel her face flushing, but she feigned a nonchalant shrug. "Don't believe everything you hear or see."

"Oh? So I should disregard that five-minute kiss?"

"Sounds serious," Winnie interjected with a grin. "You timed it and everything?"

"It just so happened to coincide with a batch of cookies in the oven. It's not like I set the clock on purpose."

So much for nonchalance. So much for sensible conversation. Kass pointed into the kitchen. "There's some cooking club prep with my name on it."

"Sure there is." Rebekah laughed.

"I'm happy for you, Kass," Winnie said softly.

Kass couldn't help staring at her. How could Winnie think that, let alone say it? With her husband in the grave only two weeks?

"Al and I would have been married twenty-five years in November. They were good years. I wouldn't trade them for anything."

"But they were cut so short," Kass blurted out. "You should have had fifty years. Or sixty."

Winnie shook her head. "We can't live that way. Not for long, anyway."

Not for long? Alberto Santoro was barely gone. Didn't his widow have a right to grieve? To resent the anniversaries that would never be, the fact that her kids' future babies would never know their grandfather? To find it painful to look on the happiness of others?

Kass would wrestle with those things big time. She knew it. Winnie was a better person than her.

"Thanks for being there for Michael." Winnie turned to Rebekah. "He's struggling a lot, and I don't know what to say to him. He and Landon would only be comforted if I wept all day and all night and forgot to feed them."

"It's hard for kids," Rebekah murmured. "I'm glad Michael feels free to come to my office, and I hope the counselor at the high school can help Landon. We all handle grief differently."

"It's not that I don't cry. That I don't miss Al with every cell of my being. It's not that I'm not grieving."

"I understand."

The conversation felt private. Kass should walk away, but she was riveted to the spot. What was her secret?

Winnie glanced at her with a wan smile. "Jesus is with me, every minute. When I think how many people heard the gospel at Al's celebration of life, all I can think of is how thrilled Al would be and how he'd pump his fist. He shared Jesus with everyone he met. He lived life in a big way, and he's affecting people still."

The funeral had impacted Wesley, and he hadn't

even known Al. What about all the mourners who had? Like Dan, even.

"We act as though we have forever." Winnie squeezed Olivia tightly in her arms. "And we do, but maybe not here. We have to make the most of every moment, every day. Take no prisoners. Have no regrets. Just live and love and laugh as much as we are able."

Could Kass do that? Even in the light of Al's death, of the unstable foundation of her parents' marriage?

Where's your faith? It seemed God whispered into her soul. *Let me take care of Wesley. Trust that I'm big enough to call him into a relationship with me. To shower him with every facet of my everlasting love and invite him to love me in return. It's not your job, Kassidy. It's mine.*

The weight on her heart lifted just a little. Wesley's salvation wasn't her responsibility. And even though her dad hadn't followed through with a deep, personal relationship with Jesus didn't mean Wesley wouldn't. It wasn't up to her to judge whether it was real or because of her.

She reached out and gave Winnie a hug around the toddler. "Thank you. I needed that."

Olivia patted Kass's cheek then leaned over and left a wet smooch.

Kass chuckled around the tears that wanted out. "You're a little sweetie-pie, aren't you? Can Auntie Kass have a hug?"

The little one wrapped both arms around her neck

as Kass twirled her away from Winnie. Olivia giggled...
and Kass giggled back.

WESLEY STOOD BACK from the doorway, watching Kass
plant slobbery kisses all over the chortling baby's face.
The joy they found in each other was contagious, as
evidenced by the grins on Rebekah's and Winnie's
faces.

Had Sydney ever played with Sebastian like that?
Never mind someone else's child. If she had, he
couldn't recall it. Enough with the comparisons,
though. Sydney was gone. Kassidy was here.

Until now, he hadn't allowed himself to see what a
future with her might look like. Sure, he'd done a little
dreaming, but not so much about the parts that weren't
physical. Now he could see her in his house, pregnant
and round with his baby, showering love on that child.
Snuggled up with Sebastian on the sofa, reading stories.
Casting a fishing line into the river behind his place.
Turning to smile at him with a baby in her arms.

Wait.

That's what she was doing right now. A baby, but
not his. Not hers. She stopped in mid twirl, her dress
swishing around her knees. Her two friends turned to
see what had caused the change. Rebekah smirked. The
other woman was Al Santoro's widow.

Caught. Wesley's smile faded. He stepped toward

the kitchen. "Hi there." But his gaze refused to stay away from Kass for more than a second or two at a time. She was gorgeous, her long red hair tied back in a ponytail, freckles dotting her nose, brown eyes soft as they looked back at him.

"Hi yourself," she said softly.

"No sidekick today?" asked Winnie.

"He's at school until two-forty-five."

"Right. Like Michael. We should call the office and see if Michael can walk him over here when they get out, unless you have made other arrangements."

"Uh, his grandmother is picking him up."

"That's good then."

Wesley took a deep breath. "I'm sorry for your loss, Mrs. Santoro."

"Winnie."

He nodded. "Winnie. I didn't know your husband, but I attended his funeral. It sounds like he was an amazing man."

Her eyes seemed a little bright with tears.

He needed to get this said before she broke down completely. "I'd already been asking questions about the Bible. Myles and Tomas have been answering them. But a lot of it clicked that day. Pastor Tomas says I can count on Jesus, that He's the same yesterday, today, and forever. I've put my faith in Him to rescue me."

"Al would be so glad to hear that," she whispered. "That's all he ever wanted, was to grow God's kingdom."

The kingdom of heaven. Another question Wesley had forgotten to ask Tomas. Behind him, he heard the community center doors and voices. It would have to wait.

"We ready to start?" Catalina Romero's strident voice came from beside his elbow. "Hello, handsome. Fancy meeting you here."

How should he handle this woman? At least today she wore jeans and a shirt, even though it was open a couple of buttons too far. "Hi, Catalina."

She gave a smug grin at Kass as though she'd won a round.

That was never going to happen. Kass was a class act, and Catalina... well, wasn't. She was barely a cheap imitation.

Trudy Trenton handed off a toddler to Winnie, who excused herself into the other room as several others entered the kitchen, chatting among themselves. Wesley glanced back to see Peter give his aunt a side hug and exchange a few words with her.

Was Winnie for real? Everything he'd heard indicated yes, she was. Her and Al, both. If Wesley lived long enough, with God's grace, he'd have a legacy like that, too. A loving wife... and more. He turned into the kitchen as Kass called the group to order.

"Time to get started. You all should have received an email a few days ago with the menu inside. We've got some new flavors this time around. Marietta donated several buckets of heirloom tomatoes, zucchini, eggplant, peppers, and herbs so we're going to make pasta sauce and ratatouille. Trudy, could I start you out with prepping tomatoes for roasting? Catalina, this pile of zucchini needs chopped into chunks maybe half an inch square. Rebekah, would you mind starting the stewing meat?"

The women nodded and moved to their stations.

"Peter and Wesley, could you chop the eggplant and peppers?"

Peter gave Kass a sloppy salute in Wesley's peripheral vision, but Wesley kept watching her. Time stood still until she finally turned to a young woman named Makenna with a request for chopped onions.

"Which do you want to do?" Peter asked.

"Uh. The peppers? I've never cooked an eggplant before, so I'm not sure what to do with it."

Peter grinned. "Eggplant could easily be my favorite vegetable on the planet. It turns bitter if it doesn't get enough water, but that's never a problem with my nonna's garden."

"Marietta, right?"

"That's her. The one and only. She keeps the whole clan in line." Peter paused, biting his lip. "Losing her son, the youngest one at that, is hitting her pretty hard, though."

"What's it like to be part of a big family?"

"Pros and cons." Peter whacked the ends off a deep purple oblong. "Everyone is always in each other's business, so forget having a secret for long.

But, on the other hand, someone always has your back."

"Must be nice." Wesley sliced through a bright yellow pepper.

"Not much for family?"

"None."

Peter glanced his way with a low whistle. "I can't imagine."

There was no time like the present to settle into his new community and begin making friends. "I grew up in foster care and never knew my own parents. Don't know what happened to them. No brothers or sisters."

"Well, you can have half of mine any day of the week."

Wesley chuckled, just the offer lightening his mood.

"I hear you've been dating Kass."

"Word gets around." They'd only been out two or three times, really. At least without Sebastian.

"It does. That whole Bridgeview-is-like-family thing?" At Wesley's nod, Peter continued. "That means if you hurt her, someone will hurt you. Might be me. Might be someone else."

"Understood. You have a thing for her?"

Peter shook his head. "Nah, not really. I like her fine, but not that way, you know?"

Wesley nodded.

"So long as you treat her right, we'll all be your new best friends. Speaking of which, how's your basketball game? Lots of good weather to play three-on-three yet this fall."

"I've played a bit. Not a lot."

"Bring your son any evening you're not tied up with Kass. Presuming those exist, of course. The guys meet at the basketball court across the street, under the bridge." He thumbed over his shoulder. "There's a decent playground for the kids beside it."

It felt like Wesley had come home. His gaze met Kass's across the room and took in her soft smile directed straight at him. Yes. Definitely home.

CHAPTER 22

*A*re there h-horses? C-cows?" Sebastian peered eagerly out the window of Wesley's truck.

Kass swiveled in the passenger seat. It was fun to experience the little boy's eagerness at the idea of visiting her parents' farm. "No horses, I'm afraid. Cows, though. And three dogs."

Sebastian focused on her, eyes wide. "Three?"

She nodded. "They help round up the cows."

"Horses could d-do that."

"That's true, but my dad doesn't like to ride. He'd rather have dogs."

"I l-like dogs. C-can we have one, Dad?"

"Now you've done it." Wesley rolled his eyes, but he was grinning.

"I'd have a dog if I didn't live in an apartment above a business." Kass smirked. What would he do with that information?

"Would you now?" His gaze caught on hers. "I've never lived anywhere permanently enough to think about pets before. Other than Taz, who thankfully can fend for himself for a couple of days while we're here."

"Duke is a d-dog. We could have a d-dog like him."

"He's practically a pony." Wesley laughed. "You should ask Violet if you could put a saddle on him and go for a ride."

"Dad! Don't be s-silly."

At least Violet had settled down some with Myles back to teaching and their new family settling into the school year. She lost no opportunity to remind Sebastian she was in third grade... but stopped short of calling him a baby. With Violet, a person took the steps that were offered.

"Turn left just past those trees."

Wesley flipped on the signal light and slowed the truck. "I'm nervous."

"You shouldn't be. You met Lenore quite a few times when she was staying with Hailey and me."

"I know, but this is different. Been a long time since I did the meet-the-parents thing, and then I got saddled with Astrid and Robert."

"How can you s-saddle Gigi?"

Kass hid her laugh while Wesley met his son's gaze in the mirror. "Sometimes saddle doesn't mean for riding a horse. Oh, look. There's the farmhouse. See the dogs?"

"Yes!"

Wesley parked the truck beside Dad's old pickup. Kass reached for his hand. "You don't need to be nervous."

"Easy for you to say." He grinned at her.

Yeah, it was. She knew Astrid fairly well since they'd worked together for several weeks now, and she'd met Robert a couple of times. But they weren't the same thing as Wesley's parents. Parents he'd never known.

Kass squeezed his fingers. "Dad will love you. He's despaired for a long time that I'd meet my match."

Wesley held her gaze. "Have you?"

She leaned over a little further and brushed her lips against his. "Time will tell," she said lightly. That was no way to ask a girl a big question.

"I want to p-play with the dog."

Wesley kissed her back. "Sorry, buddy. I'll let you out now."

Her parents stood out on the steps, Dad with his hand shading his eyes from the evening sun. Kass pushed her truck door open.

"I was going to get that for you," Wesley said across the cab.

"I know." Kass ran to the old farmhouse and gave her father a big squeeze, then Lenore. "Dad, I'd like you to meet Wesley Ferguson and his son, Sebastian. Wesley, my dad, Farrell."

Dad eyed Wesley for a long moment before giving a nod. "Pleased to meet you."

Whew. She'd been... not worried, exactly.

Concerned? At any rate, she'd definitely wondered how Dad would respond.

"Hi, Wesley." Then Lenore bent and gave Sebastian a hug. "Want to meet the dogs? This one is Trinity. She's the mama of the other two."

"They have a m-mom? I don't." He tucked his hand inside Lenore's.

Kass's eyes misted at the plaintive words. She wanted nothing more — well, *almost* nothing more — than to give that little boy a big hug and promise him she'd be his mom forever. Like Lenore had done for a little girl more than twenty years ago.

"So. You've been seeing my daughter?" Dad looked between them, his gaze settling on Wesley.

"I have, sir. She's a terrific woman, and I've come to love her a great deal." Wesley's fingers threaded through hers.

"And here a few weeks ago, she told me she wasn't sure she believed in love."

Kass hadn't thought Dad heard her or paid any attention. "But you and Mom got things squared away." Or at least, close enough that Lenore had willingly returned.

Dad grunted, but his gaze swung to where his wife sat on the leaf-covered grass with a giggling little boy and two playful pups. "The women in my life are pretty serious about their faith. Now I'm a church-going, God-fearing man, but they kick it up a notch, if you know what I mean. Sometimes it's hard to keep on their good side about the topic."

Wesley tugged Kass even closer. "I never knew much about God until a couple of months ago. Hadn't given Him much thought."

Dad shook his head as though commiserating.

"But things changed. I got introduced through my next door neighbors and a few other friends in Bridgeview. Your daughter was one of them."

Dad's eyebrows hiked as he looked thoughtfully between them.

"I came face to face with my need of a savior a few weeks ago when a man in the community passed away. Got me to thinking, what would people say about me if I suddenly died like Al did. Not just that, but what would God say when I showed up at heaven's gate? Would He welcome me in, or shake His head because we didn't have a relationship?"

"So you got pulled in, hook, line, and sinker."

Wesley chuckled. "That's one way to put it. But all I can say is, my life has new purpose now. I've got peace and joy, and I don't see it going away anytime soon."

Lenore and Sebastian shared a hoot of laughter as a pup knocked Sebastian onto his back and gave his face a good lick.

Dad glanced over then back at Wesley. "Until she starts giving you grief because nothing you do is good enough." He poked his chin toward Kass. "No offense, honey, but you and your stepmother are cut from the same cloth."

"If something happens between Kass and me, and we break up, that won't change my faith." Wesley's hand remained firm in hers, no flinching. "I hope that won't happen, because this is a woman I can see loving for a lifetime and beyond. And my son adores her, too."

"You do have to think of the children involved." Dad looked at Kass. "This one took a shine to her stepmother in about two minutes flat."

Wesley nodded. "She told me. And I can see why. Lenore is a fine woman."

"She is." Dad shook his head. "I didn't mean to give you the fifth degree the minute you drove up. Sorry about that."

"It's fine. It's something that we need to talk about sooner or later, and I'm glad to have it out of the way. Want to know how sure I am, though? About following Jesus with or without your daughter?"

Dad angled his head the same way Kass did. She'd never noticed until they all but mirrored each other.

"I've been talking to Pastor Tomas." Wesley's focus was fully on Kass now. "He told me about baptism and what it means. I'll be baptized the second Sunday in October."

Kass squealed and threw her arms around him. "I did *not* know that."

"Because I'm not doing it for you. I'm doing it because I want to show all of Bridgeview — and especially Astrid and Robert — that this change in my life is real. Permanent." Wesley swept her mouth with a quick kiss. "Forever."

Forever. She liked the sound of that.

"I CAN'T THANK you and your wife enough." Wesley looked out at the crowd in Adriana and Myles's yard. "Your friendship has meant everything to me."

Myles slapped him on the back. "We're just delighted you and Sebastian moved in next door, and we could play a small part in introducing you to Jesus."

"Not to mention introducing you to Kass." Adriana chuckled as she set two more bowls of salads on the dining room table.

Wesley surveyed the fully loaded table. All this for him? It was overwhelming. The scents of casseroles, veggies, meat platters, salads, and desserts brought by a dozen or more church members flooded the air. One thing he'd learned in the past few months, his neighbors could cook.

Kass rushed in the French doors from the deck, her red hair pulled back into a high ponytail, her brown eyes warming as she caught sight of him. "Are we ready? Everyone's waiting for you." She slipped her arm around his waist and turned to give him a kiss.

He kissed her back. Now if only all those people just went home right now... no. The time to focus fully on Kass was coming, but today was not that day. He couldn't help laughing when he caught Myles kissing Adriana before she nudged him away with a grin.

Adriana beckoned to Wesley. "After you."

Kass tugged him out the French doors onto the wide back deck. Astrid and Robert sat in the shade near the gate to his yard visiting with Lenore and Farrell, only one of many small groups enjoying the lovely October afternoon.

The crowd quietened as they realized he stood waiting.

So full. His heart brimmed over with more joy and contentment than he'd ever have believed existed. For a moment, words failed him. Only Kass's warm hand firmly gripping his kept him together.

"I can't thank you all enough for coming here today." He gestured to the Sheridans standing nearby. "And to Myles and Adriana for opening their home for this party. Every one of you has impacted my life more deeply than you'll ever know."

Marietta Santoro nodded smugly, and Wesley chuckled. Winnie smiled at him, looking a little weepy herself. Peter, Marco, and the other guys sat nearby offering thumbs-ups. Everyone from cooking club was here, the staff from the bistro, and a good portion of the Bridgeview neighborhood.

Wesley swallowed hard. "You folks know how to love a man into God's kingdom. Thank you."

"How was the water?" Alex Santoro hollered.

"When I got baptized Pastor Tomas forgot to turn on the heater and we nearly froze."

"It was wet!" Wesley called back.

Everyone laughed, but silence quickly returned when he added, "That was way more than a dunk in the tank, folks. I came out of the water washed clean in Jesus, and I'm completely overwhelmed by His mercy and love. I, uh, I've never done this before. Not out loud in front of people, but can I get everyone to bow and I'll say grace? And then we can dig into this great feast you all have provided."

Sebastian slipped his hand into Wesley's at the "amen." "Hey, Dad, can me and Oren and Isaac eat on the grass?"

"Sure can, buddy." He'd correct grammar another time. For now, it was a thrill to hear less stuttering from his little guy. Astrid's speech therapist was helping, and so was simply being settled and secure... another thing to thank the Lord for.

"I'll help the kids." Daria, Oren's mom, reached for Sebastian's hand. "You boys tell me what you want, and I'll get your plates ready, okay?"

Wesley stepped aside, not releasing Kass's hand, as others headed for the food. "Thank you," he whispered.

"You're welcome — not that I really did anything."

"You loved me before it was cool." He grinned and nuzzled her nose with his own.

"So, when will be the wedding?"

Wesley pulled away, catching sight of the Santoro

matriarch sitting in an Adirondack chair nearby. "The...?"

She waved a hand. "All this kissing. Surely it means something, no?"

"You can't rush a man, Mrs. Santoro."

"Marietta."

He nodded. "Marietta. When a person has forever on his side, there's no need to panic. All will happen in good time."

She snorted. "Some are in such a big hurry always. Others think they will never be old, that they have all the time to find a partner." She wagged a finger as she looked between them. "You want to capture one such as Kassidy when you have the chance. Do not let her get away."

"I have no intention of it, Marietta." But he grinned to soften his words.

"Quit pestering people, Nonna," said Basil from beside his grandmother.

The Santoro Wesley knew the least, really. The man had been in jail for a DUI conviction a good portion of the time Wesley had lived in Bridgeview.

His grandmother wagged her finger at him. "A good woman will straighten you right around, Basil. And if that man's intentions are to be believed, there is one less good woman on the market. Don't wait too long."

Basil scoffed. "No one wants me, anyway."

"God forgives." Why Wesley said it out loud, he didn't know. "Trust me. He makes all things new."

"Well, they've got you sucked all the way in." Basil surged to his feet. "Want me to get you a plate, Nonna?"

"Please. That's a good boy."

He rolled his eyes and strode away.

Marietta watched him go. "I pray for my wayward grandson. God is working in his life, yes?"

Kass bent and hugged the older woman. "He is. We keep praying and keep loving."

"He says he is going to Seattle. That there is nothing for him here now. All eyes judge him."

Wesley imagined it could feel that way for a guy who kept on resisting God, especially with an uncle who'd recently passed away as a result of a similar situation. "I don't know him well, but I'll pray for him, too."

Wesley Ferguson. Offering to pray for people and actually meaning it? That was amazing all by itself.

CHAPTER 23

*Y*ou're gorgeous tonight."

Kass smiled at the wonder in Wesley's voice as she settled into the crook of his arm at a table near the back of the community center. The heritage brick building had been all decked out for a winter wedding reception with silver-bedecked greenery and more candles than she'd ever seen in the same place before.

"You're not so bad yourself." The guy wore a tuxedo, after all. He was amazing enough in shorts and T-shirts like when she'd met him back in August, but the tux? Sizzling hot.

He leaned closer, his sleeve brushing her bare shoulder and his breath fanning her cheek. "How much longer?"

The cake had been cut, and Jasmine and Nathan were in the process of carrying plates of chocolate caramel decadence around and chatting with their guests. As maid of honor, Kass had already offered her toast to the bride and groom. "Not long now," she murmured.

"Good. Because I've got plans." His lips touched her ear, and the feathery earring in it whispered over her shoulder.

She shivered. Not with cold, though the winter night promised to be a crisp one outside the doors. More with anticipation from the especially attentive way he'd watched her perform her wedding duties all day today. Peter Santoro might have been the best man officially at her side, but she'd been aware every moment of Wesley's whereabouts, of his handsome good looks, of his eyes following her.

A few minutes later Jasmine and her new husband waved goodbye and ran out to a waiting limo between rows of well-wishers waving sparklers. The caterers — not Kass and Hailey this time, thankfully — turned the lights up, and guests began preparations to shift the remainder of their New Year's Eve celebrations to different venues.

"Let me get your coat." Wesley's hand rubbed her shoulder.

"I should stay and help—"

"They hired people. You're free... and some of these folks are headed to my house."

"It was good of Astrid to offer to keep Sebastian overnight."

He waggled his eyebrows. "It was. She was all in when I told her about the wedding and that I wanted to host a party afterward."

From what he'd said, it would be a small gathering of friends, but he hadn't let her help prepare. She'd be too busy with Jasmine's wedding, he'd said. This would be his event.

Most of their friends had already left before Kass made it out the door to Wesley's waiting truck. He'd started it a few minutes before to bring the interior temperature up a bit but, even with her coat, it was still nippy.

"So that was a nice wedding." Wesley glanced across the cab as he put the truck in gear. "What did you like about it?"

What kind of guy question was that, anyway? "Not bad for the time of year. I'm surprised Jasmine didn't want to wait until spring or summer. She's such a nature lover I always thought she'd be married outside." Okay, maybe Kass did have an idea or two why her friend hadn't wanted to put off the wedding for another six months. She'd waited eight years for Nathan as it was.

"I guess there are pros and cons."

"I'm sure." She hesitated. Should she ask him about his wedding to Sydney? Nah. She didn't even want to know.

"A winter night is cozier." He lowered his voice. "More intimate."

Kass shivered slightly at his tone. There wasn't

much, if anything, in this world more intimate than a wedding... or at least, what came afterward. Not something she should be thinking about, but it was hard to keep her mind from going there when she'd spent so much time with starry-eyed Jasmine in the past few weeks.

They came around the final corner to see several cars in front of Wesley's house and lights on inside.

"Oh, I'm sorry I made you late to your own party."

"Not a problem. I told them to go on in, since it's so cold outside." He crinkled a grin her direction. "I'm not Adriana. I don't have to orchestrate every minute, even if it's at my place. Now sit tight and let me come around for you."

She waited, gazing at the white twinkle lights draped from the eaves of his house and surrounding the windows on the street side. The blinds were closed, but she could see shadowed movement inside. She didn't even know for sure who all he'd invited, even from the cars. Besides Hailey — she knew that.

"Ready, sweetheart?" Wesley helped her out of the truck and took her arm. The sidewalk around to the back had been shoveled and sprinkled with deicer. He pushed the door open and ushered her inside.

"We're here!" she called out.

Scuffling noised came from the living room beyond the kitchen and then the strains of Randy Travis singing *Forever and Ever, Amen* filtered out.

Kass turned to Wesley. "Done with Christmas

carols already? I didn't peg you for a country music fan." In fact, the station he'd cranked on the trips to Galena Landing had a distinctly pop rock vibe.

He said nothing, just grinned as he slipped her coat from her shoulders and hung it along with his own.

It didn't sound like much of a party in the other room, other than the music. Why was everyone so quiet? Maybe they'd already laid out a board game or something. She crossed the kitchen and rounded the corner into the living room then stopped dead in her tracks.

A dozen people blew party horns toward her.

She pivoted to find Wesley, but he wasn't there.

Wait. He was on one knee, holding out a small box, his gorgeous blue eyes focused tight on hers. "Kassidy Jane North, I'm going to love you forever, and I want to spend every minute of that with you."

Kass pressed one hand over her mouth and the other against the doorframe, praying it would hold her upright.

"I need you, and my little buddy needs you, too. Will you marry me, Kass?"

She glanced behind her.

Everyone stood frozen in time as Randy Travis crooned his promises. After a few seconds, Hailey shook her head. "Put the poor boy out of his misery already. Say yes!"

Kass fell on her knees in front of Wesley, her sage green gown billowing out on the floor around her. She clasped her hands around his and looked deeply into his eyes. "Yes, Wesley. I love you. I'll marry you."

Party horns squeaked. Applause sounded. Probably the music continued as Wesley tugged her to her feet. Kass couldn't be sure and didn't much care. Not when her beloved gathered her close and kissed her thoroughly, claiming her as his own in front of their gathered friends.

After a long, blissful moment, he leaned his forehead against hers. "I'll love you forever and ever."

"Forever and ever, amen," she whispered, and kissed him again.

Raindrops On Radishes

— An Urban Farm Fresh Romance 6 —

VALERIE COMER

CHAPTER 1

Raindrops on Radishes
An Urban Farm Fresh Romance 6

"There's a man in the backyard." Sadie Guthrie peered out the round window in the back stairwell, clutching her cell phone to her ear. "Why would someone come into my yard uninvited?"

"What's he doing?" Denae asked. "I mean, if he's walking toward the door..."

"He's not." Sadie shifted a little. Maybe her vision was obscured, since the small window was fitted with circling stained-glass bluebirds in a sea of slightly wavy clear glass. "He's... digging?"

"You're kidding, right?"

Could the distortions mess up her eyes that much? Not possible, but having another peek from the kitchen window before she hung up on her best friend and called the police seemed like a good idea. "I'm going downstairs to get a better look."

"I'll stay on the line. Because what if he's hiding a body there? You might be his next victim."

"Or you might read too many mysteries." Sadie entered the kitchen and angled a look out the window above the sink, taking care to stay in the shadows in case the man looked up.

"You okay? Is he still there?" Denae's voice prompted.

"I'm okay. And he's definitely not digging a hole deep enough for a body. It looks more like he's... gardening."

"Did you say *gardening*?"

"Yeah. But who does that in someone else's yard?" There'd been signs, though, when she bought the place. Denae and her cousin had hurried Sadie through the house when they came to clean out their grandmother's lifetime of collections.

Sadie had signed papers on the spot. This was exactly the sort of heritage home she'd been looking for all over Spokane, Washington. That she'd be only ten minutes from her office downtown while living in a quiet neighborhood backing a steep hillside had sealed the deal. She didn't even mind the throwback kitchen, which didn't match the era of the house one iota. It wasn't like she cooked, so how bad could it be?

Her brain clicked that Denae rapid-fired questions

at her. "How old is he? How is he dressed? Is he looking around to see if he's being watched?"

"Um, he looks maybe thirtyish? Dark curly hair brushing the collar of an old denim shirt. Scruffy jeans."

"I guess mass murderers can start at any age."

"Denae. Stop it. You're scaring me."

"No, I'm protecting you. Has Grandma's landline been disconnected yet? Because I'll stay right here while you call 9-1-1."

"They removed the wires this morning."

"Maybe you can go out the front door and make the call from a safe place, like next door. Only what if they're in on it, too?"

"In on what?"

The man stood and stretched from side to side then leaned on the handle of a long spade and glanced around. He did look rather suspicious. Could Denae's over-active imagination be right, just this once?

"It could be a crime ring. If not murder, maybe drugs. Or maybe he's going to bury the cash or jewels from a heist and frame you for it!"

"Denae. Don't even—"

"You can't be too careful."

Decades ago this neighborhood under the bridge had been a magnet for addicts and the destitute. Sadie might not have spent more than an hour in the house before signing papers, but she'd researched Bridgeview along with every other area of Spokane in her year-long search. She'd missed an opportunity for a riverside home near here just last summer by pondering too long, and she hadn't been about to make that mistake again. Not when the price was so reasonable, and the old woman's family hadn't even listed it with a realty yet.

Win, win.

Maybe.

The man turned as he looked around, a crease furrowing his brow. Even with the frown, he was awfully cute. His denim-clad shoulders were broad, his sleeves rolled up to reveal tanned muscles in his forearms. Who in the Pacific Northwest had a tan by the end of March? The snow had only finished melting away a few weeks ago.

She knew the moment he realized something was off. His gaze sharpened on the collapsed cardboard boxes beside the back door. He scanned the back of the house again, and Sadie stepped even further into the shadows lest he could see six feet back into the unlit kitchen.

Denae's jabbering faded into meaningless, rolling sounds.

He strode toward the porch.

Sadie gripped the phone with a sweaty hand. What a stupid design for a house! There was no escape from the kitchen without being in full view of that back door. She heard his footsteps cross the deck. Heard the sharp knock.

There was no place to hide. She let out a shaky breath. "Denae?"

"Are you okay?"

"I-I'm not sure. He's coming to the door. I'm going to set the phone down a few feet away and go answer it, okay? Don't leave me."

"I've got your back. If he messes with you, he'll pay. I promise I won't let your death go unavenged. Just a sec. I'll start recording."

Another knock sounded, louder this time.

"Stay quiet so he won't know you're listening."

"Mum's the word."

The door creaked open. "Mrs. Essery? Are you home?"

That had been the former owner's name. Was this guy on walk-in-without-an-invitation terms with the old woman?

Sadie tapped the icon for speaker and set the phone down on the counter, but her shaking hands missed. The device clattered to the scuffed wooden floor.

The intruder's gaze swung to meet hers.

THE WOMAN STARING BACK at Peter Santoro was definitely not Beulah Essery. She was fifty years younger, had more curves, and was a whole lot prettier, for starters.

"Sadie? What happened? Are you there? Or I'm

calling the police." A panicked voice squawked from the phone on the floor.

The woman — Sadie? — grabbed the phone. "Sorry. It fell on the floor. Hang on a minute." She straightened, her gaze never leaving his as she set the device on the counter. "Who are you and what are you doing in my backyard?"

Peter blinked. "*Your* backyard?"

Her blue eyes shot fire at him. "Yes. I bought this house. You're trespassing."

"Uh... no. Beulah and I have an agreement. She'd let me know when she was ready to sell, and I'd buy it."

She shook her head. "Beulah Essery passed away two weeks ago."

No way. This woman had to be lying. Or Peter was having a nightmare. That was it. He'd wake up in a few minutes and share the story with Alex over morning coffee. They'd both have a good laugh before Peter came next door to sow the second planting of sugar snap peas. Right?

The woman didn't seem like a dream. She looked very real with her shoulder-length blond curls, white pleated top, and navy jacket and slacks. Heels. If Peter were imagining a woman, she'd be in jeans and a cute T-shirt. He'd never come up with this business look in the middle of the night.

She must be real, then. Which meant her story might be, too.

He needed to think, because the conversation had

gotten way off script. He stuck out his hand. "I'm Peter Santoro, and I live next door, renting a room from my cousin Alex. I've known Beulah most of my life. Last I heard from her, she was enjoying an extended visit with her family in Cannon Beach."

"I'm Sadie Guthrie. Mrs. Essery's granddaughter Denae is one of my closest friends."

"Hi there." The female voice crackled from the phone at Sadie's elbow.

He gave the device a sidelong look. "Uh... hi." Weird.

"Denae and I were chatting when I saw you in the yard. She's still on the line." Sadie raised her eyebrows at him.

Like he was supposed to read some significance in that?

"Yeah, I'm a witness, so don't try any funny stuff."

Peter blinked. "Funny stuff?" What on earth? They thought he was... what? He couldn't help the chuckle that erupted.

"Not so fast, buster," the disembodied voice warned.

He held up both hands as he corralled his mirth. "No nefarious purposes. I was simply tending my garden when I noticed the packing boxes on the porch and came to check on Beulah."

A perplexed frown graced Sadie's face. "Tending your garden? This is my house. My yard."

Worry gnawed at Peter's gut. "I have an agreement

with Beulah. I care for her yard, growing fruit and vegetables, and she gets all the fresh produce she wants." One thing at a time. He'd address the purchase pact after his livelihood was secured.

Sadie took a step closer, a faint scent of vanilla tickling his nostrils. "You may have had an agreement with her, but she's dead and her legal heirs sold the property to me. You and I—" she motioned between them "—don't have an agreement. While I'm sure the family appreciates you looking out for their grandmother, the situation has changed. Your... services... are no longer needed or wanted."

"*You're* the one who doesn't understand. Beulah signed a paper."

She rolled her eyes. "I'm not sure if you're always this dense or if today is a special occasion." She pointed at official-looking paperwork on the counter behind her. "I. Own. This. Property. The prior owner's agreements are no longer valid. So I'll thank you to remove your, your shovel and your presence from my yard, or I'll call the police."

"Go, Sadie!" called the voice from the phone.

Who was that person again? Peter snatched the cell. "You're Mrs. Essery's granddaughter? Didn't she explain her wishes to her family? She promised to sell me the property." He'd let the details of the elderly woman's demise sink in later. For now, he had a garden to protect and real estate to gain possession of. Could someone be forced to unbuy a house?

"Yes, I'm Denae Archibald. Beulah's daughter Lisa is my mom."

"And didn't she tell all of you what she wanted?" She had to have. Peter was grasping at straws. He knew it, but what choice did he have? He couldn't just walk away from two seasons of hard work. From all his dreams for Bridgeview Backyards, the business he co-owned with his cousin Jasmine. They needed everything to go right this summer after dipping into their savings to buy out Jasmine's brother. Cash flow was a mere trickle until sales rose. And sales couldn't rise without produce for sale.

"She did mention that the nice boy next door had approached her about buying her out."

Peter's teeth ground in frustration. "Then why...?"

"My uncle Ted is the executor, and he was determined to liquefy all assets as quickly as possible. Sadie made an offer for the house and its contents, and Uncle Ted accepted it on behalf of the estate. Done deal."

"But you can't." There was simply no way on God's green earth that this could be happening.

"Sorry." Denae's voice held no remorse.

He'd counted on this house next door so much they'd planted perennials here. Berries. Asparagus. Varieties that required several years to establish and could not easily be moved. They'd lose the income while transplanting and waiting for new growth.

Peter didn't bother pressing the button to end the call as he plunked the phone back on the counter. Let

Denae keep listening. She wanted to be a witness? All right then. Let her witness this.

"This isn't over." He stared Sadie straight in the face, steeling himself against her vanilla fragrance and focusing instead on her blue eyes, as unyielding as his own. "I have a signed agreement, and I'll be taking it to my attorney."

At least, if he had one. Alex's kid brother was in his third year of law school. That counted, right? It had to be enough for some advice.

"I won't be hiring an attorney," Sadie informed him. "I won't need one."

From the cell phone, Denae snickered.

The nerve. Peter raised his eyebrows. "I think you will." No way was he letting on his bravado was mostly bluff. Surely the agreement would hold up. Their marketing consultant — the guy who'd wound up marrying Peter's business partner — had harped on formal, signed contracts with the various landowners Bridgeview Backyards dealt with, so they'd typed something up and taken copies around. None had been notarized. Still, the contracts proved intent. That might be enough. It had to be.

A faint smile crossed Sadie's features.

Too bad the sight of it wasn't more reassuring.

"You misunderstand. I won't need repre-sentation because I am a lawyer myself."

Peter felt the nails secure his coffin with every word.

DEAR READER...

Thanks for reading *Flavors of Forever*! I'm so honored that you chose to spend the last few hours with Kass, Wesley, and me. You are appreciated.

I'm an independent author who relies on my readers to help spread the word about stories you enjoy. Would you take a few minutes to let your friends know on Facebook, Instagram, Goodreads... wherever you hang out online? Also, each honest review at online retailers means a lot to me and helps other readers know if this is a book they might enjoy. I'd sure appreciate your help getting word out.

I welcome contact from readers. In fact, I've got a readers group on Facebook where you can chat with me and other fans about my stories!

At my website, you can contact me via email, read my blog, and find me on social media. You can also sign up for my newsletter to be notified of new releases, contests, special deals, review opportunities, and more by email!

    - Valerie Comer

    www.valeriecomer.com

    http://valeriecomer.com/subscribe

    http://valeriecomer.com/FBreaders

ABOUT THE AUTHOR

Valerie Comer lives where food meets faith in her real life, her fiction, and on her blog and website. She and her husband of over 35 years farm, garden, and keep bees on a small farm in Western Canada, where they grow and preserve much of their own food.

Valerie has always been interested in real food from scratch, but her conviction has increased dramatically since God blessed her with four delightful granddaughters. In this world of rampant disease and pollution, she is compelled to do what she can to make these little girls' lives the best she can. She helps supply healthy food — local food, organic food, seasonal food — to grow strong bodies and minds.

Valerie is a *USA Today* bestselling author and a two-time Word Award winner. She is known for writing engaging characters, strong communities, and deep faith laced with humor into her green clean romances.

To find out more, visit www.valeriecomer.com where you can read her blog and explore her many links. Valerie also blogs with other authors of Christian contemporary romance at www.InspyRomance.com.

Why not join her email list where you will find news, giveaways, deals, book recommendations, and more? Your thank-you gift is *Promise of Peppermint*, the prequel novella to the Urban Farm Fresh Romance series.

http://valeriecomer.com/subscribe